P9-CEM-096

ONE MORE CHANCE

Lightning crackled, and the silhouette of Adele slowly walked away with Mom's arm around her shoulder. Adele. One hellish minute had changed her world. She believed in me, counted on me, and I had failed her, let a monster lay hands on her. I could make Addy's life right.

I could stop both Maydays from happening.

"Take me back," I whispered. "Real back. Real everyone-can-see-me back." I glanced over my body. "Take me back to April. When I was thirteen. Just before Mayday."

Sadie raised her eyebrows. "You want to be thirteen? That would place you in middle school? What was so important?"

"You gave me a choice. I chose. Can you do this or not?"

"Spunk you never lacked." Sadie thought a moment. "April of your thirteenth year? So be it. You'll be needin' these." She handed me newly knitted mittens. "Minnesota can still be cold in spring. Now go on. Best hop in back and get changed."

MAYDAY

JONATHAN
FRIESEN

speak
An Imprint of Penguin Group (USA)

SPEAK
Published by the Penguin Group
Penguin Group (USA) LLC
375 Hudson Street
New York, New York 10014

USA * Canada * UK * Ireland * Australia
New Zealand * India * South Africa * China

penguin.com
A Penguin Random House Company

Published by Speak, an imprint of Penguin Group (USA) LLC, 2014

Copyright © 2014 by Jonathan Friesen

Penguin supports copyright. Copyright fuels creativity, encourages diverse voices, promotes free speech, and creates a vibrant culture. Thank you for buying an authorized edition of this book and for complying with copyright laws by not reproducing, scanning, or distributing any part of it in any form without permission. You are supporting writers and allowing Penguin to continue to publish books for every reader.

THE LIBRARY OF CONGRESS HAS CATALOGED THE SPEAK EDITION AS FOLLOWS:
Friesen, Jonathan.
Mayday : a novel / by Jonathan Friesen.
p. cm.
Summary: "Seventeen-year-old Crow has devoted her entire life to protecting her sister Adele—even putting her own life on the line. But when an attempt to rescue Adele from a suitor puts her soul into a limbo between life and death, Crow is given a chance to inhabit a loaner body to go back and change the past"—Provided by publisher.
ISBN 978-0-14-241229-9 (pbk. : alk. paper)
[1. Soul—Fiction. 2. Sisters—Fiction. 3. Coma—Fiction.] I. Title.
PZ7.F91661May 2013
[Fic]—dc23
2013017913
Speak ISBN 978-0-14-241229-9

Printed in the United States of America

1 3 5 7 9 10 8 6 4 2

TO LOST SOULS EVERYWHERE

Let's start with where I'm not.

I'm not in a dark tunnel walking toward a bright light.

I'm not drifting toward heaven, looking down on my body.

I'm seated in the front of an ambulance—alone—waiting. I'm not sure if this is a normal rest stop before the long trip; I've never died before.

A series of notebooks spreads across the dashboard. On the cover of each, the scrawl of green permanent marker. Josh, Gertrude, Jordan—each tablet has a name. Mine simply says Crow. There are no instructions, but when I saw the pen that rested on the driver's seat, I knew what my notebook was for.

I'm writing out my life. Maybe someday everyone has to give an account. Maybe this is how it's done. Maybe this is how secrets leak back from the other side, and end up newspaper headlines. Addy, please, if the insanity of my last weeks reaches your hands, read it through with an open mind. Don't be afraid of what you'll discover. I want you to know it all.

I didn't love you well, sis. I didn't know how. You have every right to remember me as a freak or a philosophical head case. Both are true. But for me, it's time to own up, and as I don't know where this ride ends, this may be my last opportunity.

I know you don't like reading Nietzsche, but he got this one right: "The complete irresponsibility of man for his actions and his nature is the bitterest drop that he who understands must swallow." It's hard to accept what I did, harder still to accept how I hurt you and the others. So after you read this, please share it with all those concerned.

Especially Dad.

Here's what I did.
Here's why I did it.
I'll start at the beginning, which, of course, was my end.

Please remember I loved you,
Crow

CHAPTER 1

THE THOUGHTS OF C. RAINE

A bad beginning makes a bad ending.

Euripides, *Aeolus*

I DON'T RECALL MY FIRST TRIP TO REGIONS HOSPITAL.

From information pieced together later in life, I know it was an odd, but otherwise unremarkable, visit. Dr. Ambrose displayed a curious affection for the forceps, and tugged me, the raven-haired girl, from Mom, who likely would've approved the use of a tow truck had it separated the two of us quicker.

Dad's role was much smaller. Unstable man that he was, he fled Mom's birthing screams and spent most of her labor pacing and muttering in a lobby. Upon news of my arrival, he returned to perform a birth's supreme act of symbolism. He muscled dull blades through the purplish umbilical cord, forever severing the maternal bond.

"Your father was so proud of you . . ." Mom said many years later, before rubbing her face and turning away. "For one hour. It didn't take him long to decipher what type of child you would be. Wailing always did him in." Here, she paused to offer an exaggerated sigh. "You know how fragile he was."

Actually, I did not. Dad was my hero until the day he left, his return the object of my hidden hopes long after. But Mom's sigh achieved its desired shaming effect.

By all accounts, I cried for twenty-six hours straight. Never had those scrubs encountered a child with so much will in the lungs. The newborn nursery staff housed me in a torture chamber renamed the Circumcision Room, where I became the world's youngest boarder. It boasted soundproof walls, and my internment there was a nursely attempt at mercy toward other, less-vocal newborns. Mom visited at feeding times. Dad peeked in then quickly fled my noise. And somewhere, in between all those comings and goings, a name appeared on my bassinet: Coraline.

It's a pretty name, and Dad alone used it. One of the scrubs in the nursery saw to that. She removed my pink hat, stroked my black hair, and sang lullabies to her "Little Crow." Mom heard her singing and my cawing, and the name stuck. I entered life pre-nicked.

On Day Three, the hospital evicted me. Dad pulled the

Volkswagen into the turnaround. Mom received her ceremonial wheelchair ride to the curb, her arms laden with flowers and balloons. . . .

But no child. I followed at a distance, borne by an anxious scrub, no doubt concerned that a parental escape was somehow in the works. She stuffed me into my mom's arms; Mom stuffed me into a car seat; and after all that stuffing, the Raines brought home their colicky baby, who owned a scream that shredded any remaining hope of their marriage's survival.

—

I don't believe my final hospital visit was as commonplace.

Train-car collisions were rare. That Will survived the collision was rarer still. My prospects, as driver and recipient of the impact, were much more tenuous. Using the persuasive doctor jargon Dr. Ambrose must've learned in medical school, he became more forceful by the day as he discussed my bleak outlook with Mom.

"Your daughter will not wake up. Her brain activity is below the baseline for recovery. The humane choice is to let nature take its course." Read into those comforting words: Flip the switch. Pull the trigger. Kill your girl.

As much anger as I carried toward this doctor, it struck me that he was in a surreal position. He had brought me screaming into the world. Eighteen years later, he had the chance to silently usher me out.

Here I need to ask my sister. Did you wonder—I know you did—where I was when I was hooked up to the machine? When the beep was steady? When the ventilator in my mouth sucked and filled, sucked and filled, and the screen that searched for life said Death had come?

Ambrose and all the scrubs spoke in hushed voices, scared that Lifeless—an apt name for my body—might overhear. They stared and spoke in mock horror, as if they couldn't believe it had happened.

But even more than that, they wondered, like you wondered, where I really was.

I'll tell you.

I was right there in the room. Did you ever sense my presence? Could you feel my gaze?

I trailed Nurse ICU to the employee exit, listened to her and the other scrubs giggle and laugh and joke about the Unthinkable:

"Why don't they pull her plug?"

That's when I spit in her double latte. Did she taste it? Likely not. I tasted nothing either.

How does a disembodied soul spend its days? This you'll soon see. But initially, there was plenty of time to sulk, and question.

What is a soul, anyway? You'll remember how I spent time thinking about that, how the concept of an invisible center bothered me. I never became comfortable with the idea of a soul.

Descartes didn't either: "But what then am I? A thing that thinks. What is that? A thing that doubts, understands, affirms, denies, is willing, is unwilling, and also imagines and has sensory perceptions."

Foolish man. As if senses are nothing.

One thing I knew: to a soul, to me, senses were everything. They were what fresh air and blue sky are to a prisoner, what running and leaping are to an invalid.

The numbness of a floating soul—how do you bear the emptiness? It was a stupid philosophical question until I experienced it. Then, the desire for touch overpowered all else and consumed my every thought.

Except for one. As I stared at Lifeless, I still felt the connection, and the idea sickened me. An invisible umbilical cord stretched from it to me—wrapping around my midsection. Not even Dad's shears could cut me free. Though I tried to leave its room, I couldn't stray far from Lifeless.

And when it dreamed, I dreamed.

And the dream was always the same.

CHAPTER 2

THE THOUGHTS OF C. RAINE

*The hour of departure has arrived and we go our ways; I to die,
and you to live. Which is better? Only God knows.*

Socrates

"CROW?"

This irritated. She said my name like a question. As if my
little sister needed permission to enter its room. As if Lifeless
could even answer.

Adele looked good—tan to my pale, healthy to my bony—
though I do wish she would've asked to borrow my jeans.

This time, I might've said yes.

"Hi, Addy," I rose from the corner and moved nearer. "I'm
over here."

I heard me. The mirror reflected me. The chair supported
me. Dead things knew I was there.

"I came alone." Adele quietly rounded its bed. I stretched
out my hands and closed my eyes and stilled for Adele's

embrace. She entered my arms. I tensed, then relaxed. I turned and saw Adele behind me. She had passed . . . through.

I never got used to that.

"*He's* not here," Adele whispered. She swept the chair toward the bed and the hair off Lifeless's cracked lips. "You look better today." Sis forced a smile, but it couldn't stay. "Maybe a little more color?"

She paused and her head bowed. "Won't you wake up?"

Tears fell and Addy draped her body over Lifeless and I hated it all the more—the stupid thing was comatose but still received the touch I wanted more than anything in this world.

Adele visited every day. She's the only one who did.

And after what I did to her . . .

I walked around the bed and hugged her from behind.

"Will is recovering fast. He's sitting and talking." She sniffed and swiped her eyes with the heel of a hand. "The doctors say he'll probably be released in a week. So that's good."

I straightened. "No, it's not. He has plans for you. Mayday plans. The same ones Jude had when we were little. Stay away from him." I folded my hands. "You know, I was driving him as fast and as far away from you as I could, but now I . . . I can't protect you anymore."

Adele didn't know how much time I spent in Will Kroft's room, yanking at his IV drips. Harsh, I know. But what do you do to guys who want to destroy the one thing on earth you've sworn to protect?

My sister hummed, the same song I had hummed to her when the nights were bad and sleep was hard to find. I stared at Adele, her hand on its cheek, and marveled.

Why do you still come?

Not for confessions. Other people did that. Whether or not they knew me. People told Lifeless everything, like she was an ancient priestess. They dumped their trash on the vegetable, and left feeling light and free.

Things I learned since the train clipped my car:

- The harshest, most feared girl at Central had exactly zero real friends.
- Adele hated me, for about one week.
- The double-latte night nurse cheated on her husband.
- Jude, my stepdad, had Mom so blinded with his therapeutic excuses that she couldn't see his hand destroying us all.
- The first of May is out to get me.

Adele paused midsong and whispered, "You really need to wake, sis. Jude is starting to talk about some things. You just need to wake soon 'cause the doctor . . ."

"Go on, say it." I exhaled slow. "We took the elevator together yesterday. Ambrose needs the bed. He needs the room. Lifeless is a vegetable."

"He says you don't think, but I don't believe him."

"He's close to right. It dreams though, if that counts."

Adele said nothing more. She rested her head on the bedrail and held its hand. In this moment, Adele gave me the greatest gift. The gift of pain. A deliberate rend that tore me in two, though there was no me to grasp. How clear it was: Adele was both my kite and anchor in this world. The one person I would die for, and the only one I could not leave.

What I would have given to feel her hand, to believe that beyond this hospital room, that chance might come around again.

I plopped into the recliner and watched Adele's face. So innocent. She was worth it. My disembodied state . . . She was worth it all. Adele stood and kissed its forehead . . . and I gasped. Whatever air souls breathe grew thick. That was my kiss, the one meant for me. I jumped up to receive mine.

"Addy? Please, don't go."

She left. I followed a short distance down the hall, reached the nurse's station and froze.

A force gripped my middle, and I yawned. I raised my hands and let it pull me back toward Lifeless.

Time had taught me there was no escape, no weapon to fight this foe.

My eyelids grew heavy.

I knew what came next.

We're starting to dream.

CHAPTER 3

THE THOUGHTS OF C. RAINE

Dreaming men are haunted men.
Stephen Vincent Benét, *John Brown's Body*

THE RECURRING DREAM BEGAN IN A FIELD, green and lush and surrounded by woods. I never actually walked through waves of tall grass, and Lifeless might have dreamed the country all wrong. Maybe peaceful glades hid broken bottles and serial killers, but if so, I liked the delusion. The field was light and joyful and felt like spring. My heartbeat quickened—scary fast—but I wasn't too worried. Lapsing into a second coma seemed a stretch.

I kicked off my shoes and ran, circling the field, feeling stronger and wilder with each step. Rabid dogs also ran in circles—the similarity was not lost on me. Sure, I could explore the woods, but I clung to every green moment.

The place calmed me, reminded me of *The Sound of Music*, opening scene, without the mountains, or Julie Andrews.

I slowed and spun and smiled and felt warmth on my face . . . and there stood Adele and Mom. We leaped like fools through waist-high grass of soft green. Mom was beautiful as the field was beautiful. She laughed, and the sound *was* music.

Such a strange sight—Mom's carefree smile. In life, I never saw it. Such a gentle laugh she owned. In life, I don't remember hearing it.

Mom also spoke. We all did. And of all the things I can't remember, these unknown words haunt me the most. Words dribble fast and pointless off the tongue throughout our lives. Useless, meaningless . . . until after. Then every word feels weightier.

I had so many questions. Did she ever believe me about Jude? Why did she blame me for so much? Was I precious to her?

I wish I could remember what Mom said to me in that dream.

Adele sprinted ahead; only in Lifeless's unconsciousness was she faster. I gave chase, and around me daffodils, yellow and brilliant, exploded the grass with color.

If only the dream ended there.

I slowed and glanced up. The sun scorched, expanded. Adele seemed happy. As if it was her first romp through the subconscious. That was Adele. Naive. Trusting.

Vulnerable.

Ralph Waldo Emerson said, "Fear always springs from ignorance."

He obviously never met Adele.

But I knew the dream's course, and my jaw tightened.

The sun. The flowers.

The dream burned yellow. Alert, slow down, use caution.

I shielded my eyes. Behind me, Dad's voice whispered, "My Coraline, look after Addy when I'm gone." I whipped around and lunged at the rustling. I crawled, blind and frantic. Though I never found him, Dad's voice alone swelled my heart. Again, he called my name. More rustling, and I swept aside a swath of grass.

A snake, coiled and black, slithered toward me.

I jumped to my feet, lifted my heel to stomp. It spoke with Jude's voice. "Where's Adele?"

"Run on, Addy!" I screamed. "Hide!" The snake slithered after my sister.

I fell to my knees and hid my eyes.

Red. The dream turned red.

Wake up, Crow, wake up!

I pinched myself, slapped myself, knowing that this would be a good time to exit, but Lifeless's subconscious held me fast.

Red lights flashed. Train-crossing lights. Fire-engine lights. Squad-car lights.

Before me, my body lay limp and bloodied in a ditch. Thankfully, the nightmare was almost over.

"Ambulances," I whispered. "Time for you to come pick me up." On cue, three sets of flashing lights rounded the curve and approached.

I strolled to the bus-stop bench across the street, the best seat from which to watch me bleed. Here is, perhaps, where it all began, for the bench was different. The KROK rock 97.5 ad no longer covered its back.

Where's my KROK? I eased down, leaned back against a new ad: CROW INSURANCE: BECAUSE YOU RARELY GET A SECOND CHANCE.

"Okay, who changed this bench?" I yelled, and slapped a hand over my mouth. *That's a new line! I'm seriously off grid.*

Sirens wailed in the distance. I stared down the street, wondering, Who are these people driving cars in Lifeless's dream? Do they know they're here? Do they drive in other people's dreams—like a second job?

Ambulance number one screamed to a stop. "First, the foggy one. Okay, that's normal. We're good." I eased back.

A thick cloud filled that vehicle. Nobody got out, nobody

got in. It seemed excessive to spring for an extra ambulance, but hey, it wasn't my dream. Well, not really.

"Now the busy one."

The second pulled up, stuffed with the grim faces of EMTs. Latte Nurse hopped out, coffee in hand. She walked by the body in the road and sneaked into the Caribou Coffee shop. Probably to meet affair guy.

"And last, the empty—"

The third ambulance slowed to a stop. It's empty. It's always empty. For forty straight dreams, ambulance three drove itself.

Not this time.

A woman sat in the front seat and knitted. She glanced toward me, waved, and smiled.

I didn't wave back.

Dream intruder. You probably repainted my bench.

I glanced around. Everything else was in place. The man cross-country skiing to my left. The bum resting against the Wells Fargo Building exhaust grate on my right.

"Hey, C."

Mel, one of my two best friends, sat down beside me, rubbing her arms. "I'm shivering out here." She peeked at me. "How you doing?" Her plasticized beauty and paranoid tilt made each conversation an adventure, which made her interesting, and worth my time.

I didn't turn. Did she sound a little cheerier than normal?

Mel belonged in the dream—she remembered her lines—but her tone was different this time. More superficial, more . . . Mel, as though she were here for her own benefit and not mine.

Steam rose from a manhole and filled the street. Five construction guys walked lazily toward my death, stopped, and blocked my view. "Hey!" I called. "Move over!"

They didn't budge, and I turned to Mel. "Have you ever watched yourself die?"

Mel exhaled. "No . . . But when you want something so badly and can't get it . . . well, that feels a little like death, I suppose."

That was new . . . that little dark moment? Even the slightest change unsettled my mind.

I craned my neck to watch a policeman rolling out yellow tape. "You know, I didn't feel anything. It happened so fast."

"Living fast. That's the story of your life. But you never deserved to end up in a vegetative state," Mel said. "Basil told me you'd toe the line and then one day, you'd slip over. Maybe that's what he saw in you. The whole living-on-the-edge thing." She paused, and her voice dropped. "Really hard to compete with that."

"I never tried to mess things up for the two of you. I didn't do anything to—"

"No, you just were. That was enough."

We sat in silence.

Mel shouldered me and pointed across the street. "Will's sure a mess. You got him good."

I peeked at my crunched car. Will lay groaning, propped against the wheel well. "Yeah." I glanced around. "Is Basil here? It'd be nice to see him again, you know?"

"You'd like that, wouldn't you?" Mel snapped, then calmed. "No, he heard you were with Will in the car and didn't want to come." Mel paused and whispered, "Why'd you do it?"

Why'd I do it? I suppose it's the only question that really matters.

I turned to face her. "The train wasn't in the plan. Getting Will one hundred miles away from Addy was." I paused for a moment. "You knew the danger my sister was in. You knew what Will was going to do to her. Everybody at school did, except for trusting Addy." I clenched my jaw. "Nobody touches my sister."

That's my last line. Here, Mel rises and walks away.

But not this time. She didn't move, and my words kept coming.

"Have you ever sacrificed a life for something you had to prevent? Have you ever loved anyone that much?"

Mel's face blanched, and her eyes grew large. "I think I have."

I need to get out of this. Come on, Mel, you're supposed to be gone.

She offered a nervous chuckle. "You didn't prevent anything, Crow."

Did you catch that? You don't say that to a friend in her most unfortunate of moments. I didn't put it together until later on. Even Lifeless knew it, dreamed it, deep down inside. But back to the dream.

"Gotta go, the dream ends here." I rose, stepped into the street, and waited for the tug, the tug that yanked me toward the middle ambulance. I'd hop in and ride toward consciousness and wake up beside Lifeless.

Time passed. The tug never came.

From inside the last ambulance, Dream Intruder gestured toward me with her knitting needle. I slowly approached and opened the passenger's-side door.

"Who—"

Adele sobbed, and I glanced over my shoulder at the scene I knew so well. She hit the policeman who held her back from dying me. Even on this day. Even after I destroyed her Will, she fought to reach me. The intruder interrupted my thoughts.

"Get in, child."

CHAPTER 4

THE THOUGHTS OF C. RAINE

Death, where is thy sting?
The Apostle Paul

I SAW *THE MATRIX.* Remember the traitor scene when Morpheus gets captured? That black cat walked by Neo, twitched back, and then walked by again. Same cat. A glitch in the program. A blip in the Matrix. In the next scene, people started hitting the floor.

An unpredictable woman in Lifeless's predictable dream provided me with many very good reasons to stay out of the ambulance. The intruder was a glitch in the program. A blip in Lifeless's matrix. Nonetheless, I obeyed her, climbed in, and shut the door behind me.

Addy, here I address only you. Do you remember Grandpa's smell? That combination of old person and Old Spice? It surrounded him, filled his house, and sent a message:

relax, you're with me. That scent filled this cab. It felt like home.

I rubbed my thighs hard. Yeah, out of habit, but more for the feel of denim, which satisfied more deeply than ten minutes of popping bubble wrap. My hands didn't stop there, but slid down onto cool leather, where famished nerves ate up the feel of the smooth seat. As I said before, sensation was light and air.

The lady didn't speak or glance my way. I did both, and salivated. She looked exactly like the woman who formed the Mrs. Butterworth syrup bottle. She was brown and content and ready to spill goodness all over your plate. That grandpa smell vanished, and the scent of pancakes swelled. Go figure.

A question wormed inside my head.

"I'm dead. Lifeless is dead. This is the end. Right?"

Her lips tightened, and she set her hands in her lap. "S'pose that doctor of yours is tellin' your mom it may be up to interpretation." She turned her head and focused on my hands, rubbing as they were. "Truth is, no. You've never been more alive."

"I'm in a dream."

"True, but dreams is just life underestimated." She nodded. "You did enter this dream the usual. The bigger question is how'd you like to leave it."

I said nothing, and she broke into a wide smile. "My name's Sadie, honey. I want to help."

This yanked out a chuckle from way down deep. The scoff rubbed shoulders with a laugh and drifted out, filled with more sarcasm than I thought possible to own. I turned away, nodded out the window. "Based on the motionless girl, it's a little late for that."

In front of us, reporters scurried back and forth, dragging their cameramen like heavily laden asses, trying to get the best shot of the reporters' smiling faces and my bleeding one. The police shoved them aside, and went back to work with their yellow tape.

"She ends up a stupid vegetable, which, after you set up some serious life support, is not a very high-maintenance condition. Believe me. You can't help." I exhaled hard. "I do appreciate it, though. So now do I get to know how you snuck into—"

"Lady! Inside the vehicle. Open up." A policeman rapped on Sadie's door, and I jumped.

Officer Dewey?

Sadie winked at me and slowly lowered the window.

———

Basil Dewey, simultaneously my best friend and worst enemy, my most and my least, told precious few that his dad was a cop. "He works for the city of Minneapolis. Like a garbage man." That's what he'd say when pressed, but I knew the truth from the beginning.

"It would ruin my reputation." Basil swung his legs from the catwalk beneath the Mississippi River Bridge. Suspended one hundred feet up and with cars whizzing over our heads, it was an awesome fifth-grade hangout. He stretched forward and dropped a stone. Far below, it clanked off a barge deck. "It's kind of true. I mean, Dad does deal with everyone else's trash, you know? Besides, if your dad's a policeman, it's like being a preacher's kid."

"Is that bad?" I tossed a stone toward the boat. Miss.

"I don't know, what do you think?"

I drew my legs up close. "I think you have a great mom and a cool dad, and who cares what they do."

Here he paused, leaned over, and we bumped shoulders. "You know, if we were married, they could be your parents, too."

Yes, he said that.

"You're an idiot." But those were just words. Already at ten, I couldn't imagine life where he wasn't.

As years went by, Basil's dad also kept his cophood hidden, relishing in his secret identity each time he broke up one of our parties. "Do your parents know where you are?" he'd ask Basil.

"No sir," Basil would reply. "And I'd appreciate your not telling them."

Dewey's eyes twinkled, and then hardened. "I'll need to

take you in, son." Basil always left our gatherings in cuffs. Dewey marched him to his squad and threw him in back. Unaware that Basil's police escort ended at his own front door, our classmates ascribed to Basil hero status.

The playful interchanges forever earned Officer Dewey my respect, a fact unchanged when Basil told me he'd later been tazed three times for consumption in the comfort of his own home.

How I would have liked to see that. . . .

"I have no need of this ambulance," Officer Dewey huffed. "Move 'er out."

"In time," Sadie reached out and cradled the man's cheek in her hand. Dewey pressed his head against it and closed his eyes. When next they opened, Dewey tipped his hat and marched away.

"What did you do to him?" I quickly covered my cheeks, peeked at Sadie, and then dropped both my gaze and my hands. "He didn't see me." I had wanted him to so bad, even if it would have meant a good tazing. "I'm still nothing. It's not real. I feel me, but I can't feel any of this." I reached toward her wool mittens. . . .

Rough and scratchy to the touch. So were Sadie's fingers. I stared at the woman with wide eyes.

"Life feels good, don't it?"

"What do you know about my life?" I drew back my hand, held it up in front of her face. "Don't answer. It doesn't matter. Any minute this dream will end, and I'll wake up beside Lifeless and—"

"Shoot girl, you there right now." Sadie pointed toward the ambulance's dashboard, grabbed her needles, and started a slow knit.

I leaned forward, squinted at the mounted display; the hospital room came into focus on the screen. The cheating scrub placed my mirror back in the bedside drawer, twisted off her wedding ring, and strutted out of the room. No question about who planned to pick her up.

There lay Lifeless, her monitor beep steady, the all-done tone of a microwave. Adele stood reading aloud.

"If you need volume, hit that bottom—"

"I know where she is in the book," I said. "I've read Plato's *Republic* before. Adele does a good job. I mean, philosophy isn't her thing— What is that?"

Faint, like a whisper, a shadow slumped against the wall. Gnarled and disfigured, its eyes were closed, and I turned away.

"Hard takin' that first look, isn't it, dear?"

I shook my head. That thing was in my corner.

"So, yes, Coraline, that be what you look like, your soul anyway."

I had no words. As mentioned, I'd spent plenty of time reading about souls, whether they exist, why they exist. I had never until that moment given thought to their appearance. Weeks before the crash, I came to the conclusion that the soul is the truest part of you. Knowing that was my working definition, you'll understand the magnitude of her statement.

I'd always been beautiful. But a beautiful shell with a hideous-looking soul? My hands shook because it fit. It was possible that the truest part of me was hideous. Sadie was messing with core definitions.

Don't screw with my core definitions.

"No, that can't be my soul. I'm right here."

"Yes, child, you are. But there's much more to you than soul. This would be the part to understand: right here, right now, you are a soul-mind. Your body has a mind with choices, wishes, and dreams. Your soul does, too. But your soul-mind don't come to be aware until your body's mind falls asleep." She shook her head at the gruesome thing on the screen. "Which you done. It usually takes another to show you the shape of your true self. That be one of the reasons I'm here. That poor thing is what you look like, all right. Quite a sight.

"Anger sure can twist a soul."

I peeked in the rearview and stroked my face, the pretty one. "But I look like I used to, before."

"Yes'm. We do return folks to their physical form inside the vehicle." She touched her own face and adjusted a slouching bonnet. "Aids the conversation."

"This is absolutely crazy." I lifted the door handle, and paused.

Dream's end. I can't watch.

The final moments of the dream proceed as follows: Mom arrives on the scene and rushes toward Adele. There's hugging and weeping, at least from sis. Mom's face is stoic. Like she saw this every day. Like trains clip my car and knock life from my body on a regular basis.

Like she expects this, wants this.

There in the ambulance, filled with unexpected fury, I could not keep silent.

"It's me!" I lowered the window and stuck my head outside. "That thing is me! Cry, Mom, dammit!"

Sadie's hand landed soft and weighty on my shoulder. "You come to your crossroads, Coraline." She set her knitting down on the seat and glanced at my mom. "There's no figuring out some people. No makin' sense of that mom of yours. But honey, best a person can ever do is understand themselves." She checked her watch. "I need to make my rounds, so it's come time to give you your choices."

"Choices," I repeated, wiping my eyes with the palm of my hand.

"Ever wondered why that first ambulance is foggy? You'll find out someday. That be where your soul will end up. For good or ill. It'll take you on to your future." Sadie tapped her fingers on the dash. "I wish they'd tell me what was in there, but I don't know. I do not know. Maybe someday." She stared in silence, and then cleared her throat and pointed straight ahead. "You know where the second leads. Right back to the hospital room. Back to now."

"I get it. Future, present." I shifted in my seat. "And you're the Ghost of Christmas Past."

Sadie didn't laugh. "You *can* relive your life. You have a second chance. It's called your walkabout. It's one of the benefits of being stuck in the middle, your body's mind asleep and your soul's mind wide awake. As long as your body dreams, you're free to move in time, whenever you'd like. Her voice slowed. "But when Lifeless's dream ends, your walkabout is over."

"Dreams last only a few minutes, right?" I stared at Adele. "What difference could I make in a few minutes?"

"One minute can change the world." Sadie peeked at her watch. "You know that."

Outside, rain fell. A straight-down rain without wind. It should've stopped. That clearing sky was normally the last glimpse I had before waking. This time, the heavens did not break. The downpour grew so intense, I could no longer see the scene through the windshield in front of me.

I patted Sadie's shoulder. "This has been a nice diversion. It's been weeks since my last conversation. But I have a packed ambulance to catch." I exhaled hard. "I'm sure you'll be here next time around."

Sadie grabbed my arm. "You leave, and your roads be chosen for you. You want a say? This is your last chance."

Odds are, there was nothing true to this dream. Sadie didn't exist. Lifeless's subconscious had simply stretched a bit further than normal and used its few remaining vegetated cells to think this up. But that obsessive knitter pressed the one button I had left.

Choice. Any choice.

I couldn't risk leaving one behind, even one in a dream. I couldn't risk more hellish boredom.

Safe.

Eternal.

Lifeless.

Lightning crackled, and the silhouette of Adele slowly walked away with Mom's arm around her shoulder. Adele. One hellish minute had changed her world. She believed in me, counted on me, and I had failed her, let a monster lay hands on her. I could make Addy's life right.

I could stop both Maydays from happening.

"Take me back," I whispered. "Real back. Real everyone-can-see-me back." I glanced over my body. "Take me back to April. When I was thirteen. Just before Mayday."

Sadie raised her eyebrows. "You want to be thirteen? That would place you in middle school? What was so important?"

"You gave me a choice. I chose. Can you do this or not?"

"Spunk you never lacked." Sadie thought a moment. "April of your thirteenth year? So be it. You'll be needin' these." She handed me newly knitted mittens. "Minnesota can still be cold in spring. Now go on. Best hop in back and get changed."

"My clothes seem to fit fine."

Sadie ignored me and picked up a spool of yarn. "What shall I make next?"

"You know? That's fine." I patted her shoulder. "You just knit. I'll crawl into the rear of this ambulance and—"

A young girl rested on her back, her eyes closed.

"Sadie? There's another girl back here."

"Her name's Shane." Sadie crawled back beside me.

"I don't really care what her name is. Why is she here?"

"I told you. You a soul-mind. Outside this ambulance, you return to your soul's form, which I don't think you want to be wearing right now. If you're going back, if you want to be seen, you'll need a loaner."

"You stick my soul into this dead body?"

"Think of her as your shell. Shane's long since moved on. She's been a reliable loaner for a time. We snatched her years ago a moment before . . . never you mind. Each time we use the container, we make a few visual changes."

I pushed my hand through my hair, exhaled long and slow. "But this is a dream. I got here from a dream."

"Oh, girl. Everything real starts with a dream. You've forgotten yours, I know. Your gift for words, for scratchin' out stories and poems, you long done sacrificed up every dream you had for that sister of yours. I don't blame you. Someone you loved asked you to. Someone you really should get to know."

Sadie opened her hand. "A souvenir for your trip." She dropped my locket onto my palm. Besides his books, the only gift I kept from Dad.

The only thing I couldn't throw away.

I stared at the gold heart, which held a picture of Dad and me. My chest tightened, but I didn't figure soul-minds could have heart attacks.

"I can't open that. Every time I see his face, I feel I let him down. He asked only one thing of me, and I couldn't protect her, I couldn't and I didn't." I dropped it on the floor. "I don't want it."

"Oh, you will." Sadie bent over and picked it up. She

flipped open the clasp, and brilliant green light shone from inside.

"Remember the colors of your dream?" She tucked the locket in Shane's pocket. "We try to make things easy, so your walkabout follows the same concept. Keep the locket in mind. When this here green turns to yellow, your walkabout is nearly half over, and you better get a move on. When the locket turns red, you's almost out of time. When it fades to black, your chance to change the past has ended."

Sadie sighed. "But don't you worry none. I'll peek in on you from time to time. Now, remember, child." Her face grew stern. "This is not Adele's walkabout. It's *yours*. I'm sending you back so you can change you. I'm not sending you back for Adele. She can take care of herself. No bitterness in that girl." She squeezed my arm. "Can't yet say the same about Coraline."

Yeah, right. Adele needs me. You don't know what happened.

"Now lie down on this here cot and take Shane's hand."

I grimaced. "I'm not thrilled about touching a dead girl."

"You never had no problem trying to touch Lifeless, and she be mighty close."

I paused. Sadie grabbed my hand and Shane's hand and pressed them together. She bent down and kissed my forehead.

"Good-bye, Coraline."

CHAPTER 5

THE THOUGHTS OF C. RAINE

Every time you wink the stars move.
The Selected Writings of Ralph Waldo Emerson

I SLOWLY OPENED MY EYES. I was not in an ambulance—the world was unfamiliar—but in my confusion, I recollected this scene:

Falling, plummeting, upside down—choking on my silent terror. Though I would not let that be known.

The memories trickled in from a childhood summer. I spent the steamy months on the Kleins' trampoline.

There were two reasons for this. First off, it kept me awake. My lack of nighttime sleep required that I take extreme measures during the day to stay vertical.

The second reason was that our neighbors owned a trampoline without that ridiculous netting. Ask a kid. The bounce off the mat is fun. The constant possibility of a hard frame landing or impalement by rusted springs is the kick.

Addy and me, Joe and Whitney Klein, twins and older by a year, all risked this decrepit joyride. Shaped like a rectangle, with a sprinkler slicking the surface, their tramp was our summer.

Addy bounced small and cautious. Whitney and Joe experimented with flips.

I high-fived Death.

Joe pointed up into the oak. "Dare you." He elbowed his sister, his best got-her-now look plastered over his face.

A word about those words: *dare you*. You figure them out around twelve. You realize how stupid you look after going through with a dare. But at eleven? Survive one and you receive the fifth-grade Medal of Honor.

I quick peeked at Addy, who offered a tight shake of the head. Her fear only made the dare more appealing. I squeezed her shoulder.

"I got this one. Don't worry."

Addy stared up at the tree and then into my face. "It's too high." She whispered, "Please."

I slumped. One word from her mouth changed my intentions, drained my bravado. "Addy? I can do this. Don't say 'please' again."

She was silent.

I climbed the tree, shimmied the branch that stretched over the center of the tramp, and dangled. From the heavens, it did look a lot farther down, but a dare's a dare.

I swung like an ape, back and forth, gaining speed, and then released. I tucked and performed two complete flips. My mind exulted in my own courage, my own grace. Until I untucked and saw my position—I was landing off center, one foot just catching the edge of the mat. My other leg slipped down between the springs; my hip pitched left and landed hard on the metal frame.

I tumbled onto the ground, my back absorbing the fall's full force.

Addy's scream sounded faint, though she couldn't have been more than five feet from me. I lay motionless. My hip ached, my neck and back burned, my ankle throbbed.

"Crow's dead!" Whitney shoved Joe and fell into a blubbery heap. Joe stumbled back, turned, and ran inside.

And I laughed. Never felt so alive. There with my body on fire, for an instant, life was good.

As I noted before, sensations make the world go round.

"Sadie? Where am I?" I glanced to either side. I lay stomach to sky on the sidewalk.

Night had fallen, and my beautiful straight-down rain returned. From there on the cement, raindrops took shimmering form beneath the streetlight directly above me. They splatted on my cheeks, traced quickly down to the concrete, and joined the small stream, which carried them away.

Cool.

Wet.

My body shivered. My wool mittens hung soaked and heavy.

"It worked," I whispered. Raindrops bounced off my teeth, soaked my tongue. I would not move. Ever. This four-by-four square of cement would be my new home.

I closed my eyes and let the world have its way with me.

Footsteps neared, quickened, and a man gasped. Two fingers pressed against my neck.

More feelings. Press away!

The pattering on my face stopped. I opened my eyelids and stared at the wrinkles of Mr. Gainer. Hollock, his spaniel, befriended me with a quick lick to the temple. I brushed off the dog and wondered at this man. He had died three years ago—on my fifteenth birthday—but now stood above me, a most nimble corpse.

"Could you move the umbrella?" I asked. "I was taking in that rain."

"Good Lord!" He jumped back, landing hard on the grassy bank. This was followed by more colorful expressions and a clutching of the chest. I thought then to tell him that he would die in approximately two years . . . that on July 16, he would be found by Hollock slumped forward off the toilet with his torso in the bathtub. But would I have wanted to know the day and description of my own undoing? I let it slide.

I stood. "Mr. Gainer, it's me—"

I peeked down. It wasn't me.

"Young lady." He leaned hard on his cane and rose to his feet. "I thought— What are you doing out here?"

"I'm living? Hold on, Mr. Gainer." I felt my face. "Is anybody else in here?" All was quiet. "Any other souls? Because if there are, it's my turn right now. Got it?"

No argument.

"We need to get you home." Mr. Gainer looked around. "Do you know where you live?"

I kept feeling my body. My breasts. *That's all? Oh, wow.*

"Honestly, the last few weeks I've lived at Regions." It warmed me to tell the truth.

"This is the first thing you've said that makes sense. You must have hit your head. We aren't but a few miles from the hospital. I would drive you, but I am a mile from my home." He pulled out his cell and dialed. "Yes, it is an emergency, I have a girl here."

I swatted the phone out of his hand, Hollock flew into a barking frenzy, and I took off running. "I'm sorry about that, Mr. Gainer, really I am, but I'm fine," I called over my shoulder. "I've never been so fine." Thighs cramped, and I winced as stiff legs rediscovered their strength. "A mile from your house? I know where I am."

This wasn't completely true.

As it turned out, I was a few blocks from our cul-de-sac, but I gazed at the familiar through borrowed eyes, which changed the landscape in imperceptible ways.

Add that to the rain and the night and you'll understand why I ran around for twenty minutes before finally standing in our driveway.

"Mom's house."

Here I'll say a few words about Shane, my loaner. First, she was blond, with tanned skin, like Dad's, her light on dark opposite of the real me. Second, she could not run. This fact irritated. I'd always been fast. Shane seemed to lack the coordination I thought ordinary fare for thirteen-year-old girls. She was tall and gangly and lacked balance, definitely unable to pull off any manner of double flip.

I dug in my pocket and grasped the locket, snapped it open. It glowed a brilliant green.

Time. I have so much of it! I tossed the locket into the air and snatched it out again. The feeling of freedom that filled the green section of my dream overwhelmed. But this was better. This was no reoccurrence; I wasn't stuck in a field. I could do anything, go anywhere.

This dream belonged to me, now, not Lifeless.

It all could end differently.

Dad, I won't let you down. I won't let the Monster touch her.

I sprinted, well, lurched, around to the back of the house and checked the windows.

Jude and Mom's room was dark. Light shone through the curtains of the room Adele and I shared. All was well. I slowed when I reached the oak. A dim light glowed from the tree house nestled far above, and my heartbeat fluttered. Nobody stayed out here this late except . . .

I placed my foot on the bottom wooden rung. Dad built this strong. Known for maximum nail use and support overkill, Dad made sure that if a tornado was coming, and the neighbors headed for their basements, we'd choose to run to the tree house, at least those of us thin enough to squeeze through the opening.

First rung. Second rung.

Creak.

"Is that you, Addy? Is everything all right?"

Have you ever heard your recorded voice? No matter how attractive you think you sound, the machine steals it all, leaves you hollow and tinny. This voice was thin, thin and clear and thirteen and me.

My heartbeat quickened.

We walk as desperate men, terrified to slow down, terrified to turn around, for we might just run into ourselves. The first line from a poem I wrote suddenly felt much more than philosophical rambling.

"No." I called up. Shane's voice held plenty of terror.

Crow poked out her head, and my legs buckled. Until that moment, I felt like me. A smarter me trapped in a different shell. Now, looking at Crow, I wasn't certain who I was anymore.

"My name's Shane. Can I come up?"

"Where . . . ?" Crow frowned and bit her lip. "Where'd you come from?"

"I've been on a walkabout."

"In the rain?"

Crow stared a long time, then continued. "Yeah, okay. It's a free country."

That's so I-don't-give-a-rip me.

I climbed the rest of the way, crawled inside, and glanced around at the graffiti: phrases from books I'd read, ideas I'd worked through. All this philosophy, of course, was graced with obscenities, which is about what all those ideas turned out to be. But my gaze quickly traveled to Crow.

She pressed back against the opposite wall. Her hair was black and wild, her skin pale and beautiful. She blinked bloodshot eyes—anyone would have thought her wasted, anyone who didn't know.

Her bent knees supported one arm, while the other rested on a stack of books. Tolstoy, Ben Franklin, Nietzsche, Charles Darwin, the Holy Bible. I scooted back as far as I could. I knew a butcher knife lay behind that stack.

I breathed deep. I also knew whom the blade was meant for.

She didn't move. She stared through those unblinking eyes, but I recognized the look, the one that searched for any show of weakness.

Inside, I felt a loosening, later I would name it tenderness, toward this girl I knew so well. I remembered my appearance in Sadie's ambulance. My true self. Why had my soul hardened and twisted? When had it done so? Did it shrivel under the weight of Mom's accusations? Calcify in the silence between us? Maybe it faded along with my dreams. I could have been a writer; I had lots to say. Pain had been a good teacher.

But I didn't matter anymore. My chance to gift this world had passed. Not Adele's. She was still light and hope. Mom made that clear. . . .

"You, Crow, were the wedge between your father and me. You, Crow, are incapable of speaking the truth." This argument-ending line was powerful, and by thirteen, I was close to believing it; so, likely, was my soul.

I winced. That gnarled shadow already lived in the beautiful girl sitting among the books.

"I don't usually have visitors in my tree house." I said.

Crow's face twitched. "*Your* tree house? Have I met you?" Her hand reached behind the stack. She was nervous but wouldn't show it.

"I only meant that this is where I've been living. Guess that makes it partly mine." I let my head thud back against the wood. "I was looking at that stack of books. I, uh, noticed there's a pretty frightening knife behind it. I really don't mean any harm." I stared into Crow's face. It wasn't relaxing, a really bad sign for me. "Please." I winced. "Is your hand on that thing, 'cause one day you might miss."

Crow clenched her jaw, whipped out the blade, and flung the knife across the tiny house. It stuck in the wood about six inches above my head.

She eased back. "You've been digging in my personal affairs. That's not a good idea."

"No, not digging. Just looking, but you're right. Now that we've met, I'll be more respectful."

I reached up and muscled out the blade. It felt clunky in this foreign hand. Shane didn't have one callus, not one bruise. It was a good bet that she ran only when necessary, and she worked even less.

Great, I've been stuck in a prissy body.

Not knowing how pathetic a knife thrower Shane might be, I gently tossed the blade back between Crow's feet. Suddenly, a thought flew in, sharp and panicky.

"You're not up here much in the evening. I always have the place to myself. You're not watching Addy tonight?"

Crow frowned, lifted the knife, and ran her finger over its edge. "How do you know that name?"

Backtrack! The surest way to lose her trust would be to know too much, too soon, especially about Addy.

"When the wind dies down and your window is cracked, words, names, float up. Usually that one. I'm not trying to eavesdrop."

"Get out," Crow nodded toward the ladder.

I sighed. I took only one small step, but my toe touched her paranoid line.

"Sorry if I said something wrong. I'll go. But can I take a blanket? It might keep me dry for a little while."

"No." Crow tongued her cheek. "Stay. You can stay. Just no more family talk."

Did you just give me a second chance? I rarely trusted anyone enough to give them a first.

I leaned forward and held out my hand. "Then let's start over. Thanks for inviting me into your tree house. My name's Shane."

Crow didn't move. "Why would I need to watch my sister?"

"You said no family talk."

No response.

I swept back matted hair and let my outstretched arm fall limp to the floor. "This is a lose–lose. If I answer, you'll probably kick me out." I peeked into Crow's hardened face. There would be no escape: she was waiting. "Okay, if you sit up here, night after night, watching those two windows, watching your silhouette pace your lit-up room and watching the other room fall dark, a thick, always dark." I raised my gaze. "It makes me wonder. Why are you pacing? Never Adele, just you."

Crow bit her lip and set the knife back behind her books. I figured it safe to continue. "I can't help but question why you don't sleep. You must be staying up for a reason. That's all."

She looked at my limp hand. "I suppose it would seem strange."

"For what it's worth . . ." I crossed my fingers. My next words would push her away, or connect us forever, but I didn't come all this way for nothing, "I once guarded my sister's bed. Until the sun rose, if I needed to. Where I used to live, evil things went bump in the night."

Crow softened, and for a moment her eyes begged. When I was thirteen, I would have given anything to know that I wasn't the only girl on a silent vigil, that there was another who shared my torment. In that instant, Crow changed. Before my eyes, years fell from her like scales, and she became a girl, just a lonely girl.

"Call me Crow." She settled back, her face hardening again. "The evil that goes bump in this house is at a conference. I got questions for you, but tonight I'm too tired to care. Help yourself to the blankets." Crow blinked toward my left and closed her eyes.

I examined my spindly arms, worked by shivers. I didn't make a move for the quilts. It felt too good to feel.

Crow cracked an eyelid, peeked at the unused blankets, and hinted a smile.

"Oh, one last question." I asked.

"Hm."

"What day is it?"

"April 21," she muttered.

Less than two weeks till Mayday. Perfect.

CHAPTER 6

THE THOUGHTS OF C. RAINE

When the student is ready, the master appears.
Buddhist proverb

I SLEPT.

For most, an unremarkable occurrence, but for me, the most precious of gifts. This Shane, this tent I inhabited may have owned awkward legs and prudish hands, but her sleep was deep and dreamless.

I could not recall such a restful slumber. Ever. As I rolled, I wondered: Did everyone feel this restored by the night? I smiled and snuggled and smiled again. Sadie had given me the most perfect loaner . . . a sleeper! For the first time, morning felt good.

What a wonderful body, both refreshed and warm.

I forced open my eyelids. Covered by three quilts, I lay next to a dry pair of jeans and a Property of XXL hoodie.

I peeled off damp clothes and squeezed into Crow's black denims. I remembered the pair. Wincing, I fought with the button. I remembered them fitting.

It dawned on me that though I'd been fierce about getting back to thirteen, I had no idea what to do now that I'd arrived. School was in session, the Monster was at work, and judging on the stomach growl, Shane hadn't been fed in a while.

Warm shower. First thing I do is find a warm shower.

Crow's head popped above the floorboards. "You weren't a dream."

"That's debatable." I rubbed my face.

Crow cocked her head. "Yeah, whatever. So, do you do school or what?"

I shrugged and yawned. "Haven't for a couple weeks."

This clearly pleased Crow mightily. "So you just sit up here." Crow rested her head on her folded arms. "Like a female Tom Sawyer. You go where you want, when you want. No worries." She thought, and when finally her lips curled, I knew an idea had taken root. "Seeing as you live this dream life in the comfort of my tree house, I'd say you owe me a favor. Why don't you do school today?"

"With you?"

"With me."

"I don't see how that provides any favor. Besides, I can't." I nestled back into the pile of blankets. "They won't let you in without papers. Vaccination papers. Like a dog." I rolled my eyes.

Crow slapped an immunization record on the floor. "Copied. Should work."

"Right. And you probably need a home address," I said. "There are no house numbers on this tree."

"Tell them you live inside. I'll let you be my half sister. My dad's girl. Something happened with the other arrangement, and now you're living with us."

Yeah, that might work . . .

Crow grabbed my arm. "Don't worry so much. You frown like Addy." She paused. "I should know your last name, in case we're asked."

"Oh, um . . ."

"Owum?

"Owen."

"Well, Midway Middle School, prepare to meet my half sister, Shane Owen Raine."

I dragged down the ladder and marched at Crow's side, around the house and down the street toward the bus stop. Crow swaggered triumphant, beside her shivering, nappy-haired trophy. I knew that attitude; I had perfected it. She was up to something. I would be used, not displayed.

I sat, still and invisible, amid the mayhem that filled the bus. The kids were busy with screams and rumors and all things middle school. After all, summer approached, and even teachers conceded that learning was a memory. A bus driver's mandate? Hang on for dear life.

Then I saw her.

Yeah, it was ten rows up and from the back, but the partial view thumped my heart.

Adele.

"She has to sit toward the front, seeing as she's still in elementary." Crow cleared her throat. "But I don't mind. Gives me a chance to keep an eye on her. Sounds like you know something about that."

I nodded, and we reached the next stop. Bus brakes hissed, and Adele moved toward the aisle. She leaped up and squeezed out in front of the ten kids waiting to board. Crow and I stretched our necks and followed her as she raced beneath an underpass and set down a brown bag. Addy spun and raced back toward the bus, climbing on just before it pulled out.

"I don't know why she cares about that no-good." Crow smirked. "If Mom knew she was feeding a homeless guy beneath the Tenth Avenue Bridge, I don't think Addy's lunches would be half of what they are."

For all I remembered, there were entire chapters I'd forgotten, Addy's 10th Avenue Bridge food distribution being one of them. She always had a heart for the least and the lost.

Maybe that's why she loved me.

Maybe that's why she would one day love *him*.

We finally reached the school parking lot. The middle school kids streamed off, except for Crow, and me. Crow grabbed my hand and pulled me up the aisle. She paused at Addy's seat, bent over, and hugged her. Not a quick squeeze but an embrace. Addy's eyes closed as she soaked it in. It was our routine, and its meaning flooded my mind.

Don't worry, sis. I'm leaving now, but I'll be back. I'm always watching.

Crow stood and clenched my arm. Addy stared at me with a confused grin. I waved, she waved back, and I exited the bus. Crow peeked left then right and veered out of the flow, sliding along the front of the school and dragging me behind.

I'd also forgotten this little thirteen-year-old phase.

We rounded the school and ran across the ball fields to the vacant garage belonging to Mr. Wendallis. One yank on the side door and we were inside. Cool, dank air slugged me in the face.

"Welcome to one of my safe houses. I have a few." She dug in her pocket. "You smoke?" Crow lit up. Rebel idiot.

"I don't know." It was as close to honest as I could come.

Crow handed me one of Jude's Winstons. I inhaled deep and threw up. Crow nodded slowly and took another puff. "That'd be a no." She finished her cigarette and tossed the butt into my vomit. "That's all right. Everyone has one flaw. Just don't have any more or I'll disown you."

Crow folded her arms and sank back against the garage door. How hard I looked, how unbreakable, even at thirteen. But already stunning. Frighteningly so.

"Say, Crow, in case they ask: Where does your dad live? Since I'm supposedly his daughter and all."

Crow didn't flinch. "I don't know. None of us do. He dropped off the map." No emotion attached to her words. She offered no hint of sadness.

"Why'd he leave?" I whispered.

Crow lit up, and in the flicker of the flame, she dropped her gaze. In that moment she again looked like a young child, desperate and vulnerable. The stoic quickly returned. "Mom tells me I'm a big part of it. Some days, I believe her." She paused. "You don't learn that crap staring through a window. If you want to leave, there's the door."

I closed my eyes, and visited a different time.

⁓

"If you want to leave, there's the door!"

Five-year-old me glanced up from my sidewalk chalk in time to catch Mom shove Dad onto the front steps. He stood motionless for a long time, shoulders drooped, head slightly back. Amazing what details stick.

"And finish that garage!" Mom's voice pushed out from inside. "You know what Dr. Jude says. That roof is a symbol of provision. And if you're not willing to do your share—"

The door slammed, and Dad turned. He forced a smile my way and quietly walked toward the ladder, then eased it against the house.

"Is Mommy mad?" Addy asked.

"It's okay," I said. "Why don't you go in and give her a hug? She'll like that."

Addy ran inside, and I walked toward the ladder, yanked on the back of Dad's shirt.

"Do you want to come up?" he asked.

I dropped my chalk, Dad hoisted me onto the ladder, and together we clambered onto the roof. Tarpaper and shingles lay everywhere, and Dad surveyed the job. He plopped down, lay back, and covered his eyes.

And cried.

I lay down beside him and placed my head on his chest.

"I'm losing her, Coraline. That therapist has his hooks in her." He groaned. "Here's a quote to live by: If you're going to fight a doctor, you need more than common sense on your side. Remember that." Dad exhaled and stroked my hair. "I'm sorry, you don't need any of this on your shoulders."

I sat up. "Don't let Mommy see the doctor. Why do you visit him?"

"I don't know anymore." Dad propped himself up on an elbow. "At first we went to talk about you." He cupped my cheek in his hand. "You were one loud girl."

I jumped up and stumbled toward the ladder. "*I* make Mommy see him?"

"No, at the beginning, we went for help because, well, some kids scream. A lot. I'm not good with noise, but—"

I scampered down the rungs, Dad calling after me. "You are not the cause of what's happening. Coraline!"

But it was too late. I heard his words, and they lodged in my heart. Later, Mom would be certain they remained.

Dad tried to find me—I heard him calling for nearly an hour—but I was behind the shed hiding inside a bush, the little girl with a broken heart.

⌣

"Still with me, Shane?"

I stared at the garage door. "Sucks to be blamed by a parent who doesn't act the part."

"Yeah," she said. "It does."

"Sucks to be the only one who sees what's going in a house."

Crow stretched and sighed. "My friends—Basil, Mel— they wouldn't get that."

I forced a smile. "Yeah. It's the story of my life."

She nodded, and we dropped into a long silence. Crow walked toward me. "I'm glad you showed up."

"Well," I said, "that's my story. But I wonder, with you, maybe there was more going on between your folks than you know. I mean, marriage isn't like chemistry. Two happy people in a beaker, add a drop of kid potion, and the whole experiment blows up. I don't think it happens that way."

"I think I was there and you weren't," Crow snapped, and then rubbed her forehead and lowered her voice. "You're hard to figure out, Shane."

"There's a good reason for that."

We stepped out of the garage and walked slowly back toward the school—a long, plain-view strut in front of every window. Fashionably late, Crow practically screamed, We're tardy. What are you going to do about it?

My purpose clarified. The second year of middle school, I had no disciples. They came later, drawn out of fear. But here and now, I was Crow's first little follower.

I'm nobody's little follower. Not even my own!

"Crow, you go on to math. I'll catch you after you break out of special ed."

She slowed. "Okay, how do you know my schedule?"

My eyes widened. "It, uh, it was tucked away in Tolstoy, in the tree house."

Crow took a step closer to me. "Shane, you're freaking me out. You're either the first person who understands, or you're some clone kid planted by the government, you know, who knows my whole life." She poked my arm and my neck. "You're not one of them, are you?"

I swatted her hand away. "You watch way too many movies. Listen, after I found the knife, I thought special ed was a safe bet."

I laughed and relaxed when she did, too.

"Okay." Crow winked. "Until then . . . sis."

I walked through the front door of the middle school, my mind fixed on home. Mom's place had looked similar, but the feel was foreign. And it wasn't just the smaller trees and shrubs. Home drew me, despite the gathering storm, and it hadn't done that in a long time. From the outside, Mom's house felt warm, right. Then again, Mayday hadn't arrived.

The school's office, however, was exactly as I remembered it.

I walked in and approached Ms. Wiggle—an unfortunate name for a middle school secretary—and rang the bell on the desk.

She set down her *Good Housekeeping*. "Yes, dear."

Dear? Are you kidding?

"I need to enroll in school."

She glanced toward the door and frowned. "Your parents? Or guardian? I need their signatures and quite a bit more information." She slapped some papers down in front of me. "Are you new to the area?"

I shook my head. "Listen, you'll never get my dad in here. You won't get my guardian either. Here's the shot paper."

I reached it to her and she read aloud, "Shane Owen Raine." She handed it back to me. "I'm sorry. I need a parent or legal guardian."

"Crow's my half sister. I live with her now."

"Horrors!" Ms. Wiggle rubbed her eyes, hoping, I think, that I would disappear in the process. "One Crow's enough. Tell me there's not another half floating around." Ms. Wiggle clapped her hand over her mouth. "Wait here." She vanished into the principal's office.

I glanced around. Powder blue. Every wall was powder blue: the color of jail cells designed to drive prisoners insane. It works. Beneath the buzz of fluorescent lights, powder blue makes a person want to jump off a cliff.

Or register for school.

Wiggle returned. "Just fill out the forms as best you can, and we'll make a call."

An idea, quick and crafty, weaseled in, and I stared down

at the enrollment sheet. I fiddled with the pen, rubbed my eyes, and fiddled some more.

"Oh, for the love of heaven, not you, too. Crow barely sounds out, and you can't read either?"

I blanked my face, but my thoughts replayed the first time I'd played this game.

In school, I had been a master of deception, and no ruse proved my brilliance more than feigned idiocy. I quickly determined that my lack of sleep would not accommodate a middle school workload. Enter special education, a beautiful place where expectations and homework were nonexistent.

My present plans do not accommodate a middle school workload either.

"Let me walk you down to Mrs. Herbert. She'll be your homeroom. Room 145." Wiggle rose and peeked at me sideways. "Can you count?"

"Some days better than others. Crow's the smart one." I grinned, and followed my escort out the office door.

The halls were empty during first hour, a strange vacuum filled only with the click of Wiggle's heels.

"You will like Mrs. Herbert." Wiggle waddle-*clicked* forward. "All the kids do."

I nodded. I held nothing against her. She taught science and knew how to smile. She had treated me well, winking at me whenever she, too, dressed in basic black.

Yeah, Mrs. Herbert was kind, and I had treated her like garbage. Classic Crow.

Wiggle gentled opened the door and stuck in her head. A moment later, Mrs. Herbert squeezed into the hall, glanced from Wiggle to me.

"It's late in the year to be moving to a new school. Where did you attend before?"

"Puerto Rico?"

Wiggle coughed and set her hand on my shoulder. "This is Shane Raine, Crow's half sister."

Mrs. Herbert broke into a wide smile. "Well, that is good news. Crow's one of my favorites. She steals my outfits on occasion, but that's easily forgiven."

One of your favorites? Are you kidding?

"I'll leave you to get to know each other." Wiggle spun and *clicked* back toward the office.

Mrs. Herbert reached for the doorknob. "Are you ready?"

"Hold on. You didn't really mean that about Crow, did you? That she was your favorite. I mean, that was a fake and fuzzy welcome."

She leaned close. "'I approve of a youth that has something of the old man in him,' or in this case, in her."

"Cicero," I whispered.

"I know the others don't see it. The teachers see arrogance and insolence. But look close and it's so clear.

There's a wit and wisdom that transcends her years. Beneath the hardness, there's an old soul." Mrs. Herbert straightened. "That probably makes absolutely no sense to you."

"No, I get it. I totally get it."

She raised a brow and led me into her room, to the most predictable of receptions; it followed the three stages perfectly.

Stage One: endure zoo animal status.

My classmates watched me take out a pencil. Watched me twirl my hair. Watched me get a bathroom pass. In Stage One, they make sure you're human. They make sure you don't do anything too *out there*. They assess your value. I must have used the bathroom correctly, because when I returned I had slipped into Stage Two. Kids cozied up to me, hoping I possessed something to boost their popularity status.

"Hey, Shane. Come over here." Suzanne Wadley and four other girls fought for my attention. I chose Suzanne because Crow never cast a glance toward her.

"You're new here," she said. Many stupid remarks fill the conversations of Stage Two. "Where you from?"

"Tennessee," I lied, but it was the first state I could think of.

"Cool. How'd you end up in Minnesota?"

"I'm staying with my half sister. You might know her— Crow Raine?"

And with those last two words, I vanished into Stage Three. Suzanne smiled, turned and rolled her eyes at her friends, code for "this new girl will not be an asset." From there, you're an eyelash from ostracism, which I achieved by hour's end.

Then I saw Basil.

He stood in the hallway outside the door, and my heartbeat skipped. He was cute at thirteen and floated above the other boys' stupidity. He was cool and polite all at once, a rare commodity for a seventh grader.

I lowered my gaze and hugged my science text, pressing hard into the wall as I tried to slip by.

"Hey, new girl!"

It was time to find Crow, but one crooked smile from Basil slowed me down. "Are you really Crow's half sister?"

I started to speak but thought better of it.

"And now you're living in that house?" He stepped nearer. "With Ms. Raine and the loser—"

"Yeah," I said. "And their mom and stepdad."

He paused and broke out laughing. "That's good." His face tensed. "Don't let Crow hear you joke that way about her or Addy. You wouldn't want to see that punch line, if you know what I mean. So you're heading to lunch, right?"

"Baze!"

Mel ran up behind us and bumped into Basil's shoulder.

Mel had two things that didn't belong in this school—money and clothes. She was cute—step-out-of-a-Macy's-ad cute. The rest of us looked like we had scraped our way up from the mines.

"Oh! And Crow Number Two. Who would have thought there'd be a second C in this school?"

"No." Basil kept his eyes fixed on me. "She's different, Mel."

I tell you this comment had conflicting effects. It warmed me, I will admit. It felt good knowing I still captured his interest. But it sucked, too. Because it wasn't really me. It was Shane. And at that moment, all the time he had dominated my thoughts seemed a monumental waste of drama.

She's different than Crow. Translated: at this moment, Shane—not Crow or Mel—is who I want.

Translated: Basil is a jerk.

I turned my back on Basil and left him there calling my name. Mel's voice took over; she was working him hard. "Let her go. She's a freak, like C."

I froze, spun, and marched straight back to Mel.

"In what way, exactly, is Crow a freak?"

Mel glanced at Basil, who grinned and lifted his brows. "Yeah, Mel, explain what you mean."

She shifted her feet and squirmed beneath her backpack. "Crow's unique. That's all. It's a good thing, really." Mel scowled. "A little sensitive, aren't we?"

I caught up with Crow near the lunchroom. I would like to say she was *in* the lunchroom, but to do so would ignore the truth, so onward.

At first, I saw only a circle of kids in the foyer, near the stairs to the basement shop classes and across from the lunchroom entrance. Other fixtures off the foyer were the office, the auditorium, and the trophy showcase, all of which matter here.

I pushed through the ring. There, in the center, stood Crow, visually relaxed, her right hand opening and clenching. To the world, a girl in complete control, but I knew that hand. The same hand that readied for the knife.

Crow was ready to explode.

Facing her stood Jasmine Simone, grade eight. She was a large girl, with a mouth that filled up every inch of face space. She commanded, no, *demanded* respect. How she had not clashed with me in middle school before now was either providence, or more likely the result of my not truly coming into my own.

Jasmine circled Crow. I'd say stalked like a cat, but 180 pounds limits one's ability to stalk. Every time she reached Crow's ear, she slowed and whispered. I didn't know she could whisper.

The spectators were anxious, waiting, dreaming, to see these two titans engage in a "girl fight." Hair pulling.

Slapping. It was an embarrassing spectacle to watch, and neither fighter ended up victorious, but such events were sadly commonplace at Midway, where a hidden undercurrent of anger floated around the halls.

I squeezed my forehead between my forefingers. Think. Remember.

I came up empty, and my emptiness turned to fear, because this confrontation had never happened the first time I went through seventh grade. Jasmine never circled me. I never fought her. The next minutes, whatever they might hold, were a result of my presence, of a comatose Crow's soul-mind hopping into the body of thirteen-year-old Shane and going five years back in time.

I wasn't the rage inside the ring, but I sure as hell had set it in motion.

Jasmine stopped circling, her back to the auditorium and the trophy case.

"Everyone! To your classes. Now!" From the opposite side of the foyer, Assistant Principal Gleason stepped quickly toward the mess. "Break this up!"

Crow scratched her cheek.

"Oh, no," I whispered. "Don't do it."

"Did you mean what you said?" Crow asked, her voice so controlled, it frightened.

Jasmine chuckled. "Every frickin' word."

Crow nodded slowly . . . and charged. She drove 180 pounds straight backward into the trophy case, shattering glass and toppling thirty years of athletic accomplishment. She wasn't finished. Crow pushed Jasmine's head back with a hand to the forehead, grabbed a trophy—volleyball, for what it's worth—lifted it high . . .

I leaped forward and caught Crow's arm. She turned and cuffed me hard across the jaw, and her arm caught a shard of glass protruding down like a wicked icicle. I stumbled back, staring at the blood covering her forearm.

Crow gazed blankly at me and dropped the trophy, just as Gleason came near.

His eyes widened. His jaw dropped.

"Oh, Lord."

CHAPTER 7

THE THOUGHTS OF C. RAINE

Death is a delightful hiding place for weary men.
Herodotus

THE SCHOOL TRIED TO REACH MOM.

Apparently, she didn't answer.

As stitches were more than called for, Crow and Jasmine were taken to Regions Hospital, while I again waited in the powder blue office. Enough people witnessed the event to satisfy administration that I bore no guilt . . . that I deserved some type of commendation for coming to Jasmine's aid.

In the end, only Wiggle questioned my innocence.

"Day One. Can't read. Can't count. In the middle of a fight," she muttered, shaking her head. "Perhaps on your second day, I'll call in sick."

The principal spoke to me of duty and rising to the occasion and acquitting myself well. I sighed my way through the sermon, and when finally the dismissal gong sounded, I pointed back over my shoulder toward his wall clock.

"Can I go?"

"Yes. Thank you again, Shane. I'm sorry your first day went like this. Five days will give Crow ample time to ponder her actions, so the rest of your week should be less eventful."

"She's suspended? For five days?"

"Oh, that this would end there. If she's not sued." He spun his chair toward the window and forced his hand through his hair. "If we're not sued."

"Well, good luck with that," I said.

Five days. What a stroke of fortune! That meant more time with Crow, more time to prepare, without the hassle of classes to interrupt my plans.

I walked quickly to my locker and toward the front door.

Middle school is a strange world. Granted, my arrival somehow caused the entire flare-up, but I did the right thing. I spared Jasmine major reconstructive surgery to the face. You would think kids might flip a smile my way, perhaps nod in approval.

Instead, I walked out of school in a bubble. In front of me on the bus, an empty seat; behind me, the same. Three kids squeezed into one seat, two rows up. Their heads leaned in, while their peeking eyes made frequent trips to the new girl two rows back. I knew I broke middle school code—stay out of other people's business—but did everyone want to witness a killing? Likely so. Inside my classmates lay a secret desire to witness the macabre. Maybe that's inside most people.

It wasn't inside my dad.

———

Precious few memories lingered of the man who left when I was five. A locket here, a roof there. My five-year-old piano recital was one of those sacred few.

It was clear from the onset that my musical career would be both short and painful. Most parents encouraged their children to practice. Mom begged me to stop. Yet, my sense of duty was strong, and for hours, I pounded out "Mary Had a Little Lamb," my first recital piece.

The recital hall inside St. Vincent's Church was enormous. Surrounded by stained glass and with benches to seat thousands, I felt small and out of place. Thirty beginning-piano students and their families huddled on the first few pews, staring at the large Steinway in the hall's center.

Mom and Dad were there, and I remember the prerecital moments well. Mom worked the crowd, plastering on the smile I saw only outside our house. Dad sat quietly at my side.

"Are you nervous, Coraline?"

I pressed into his shoulder and looked up into his face. His eyes were soft. "I think I would be, too. This is a really big room, and there are a lot of strangers here. But I believe in you."

The recital began. I was the second-to-last performer, which meant my anxiety had twenty-eight songs to germinate, take root, and grow. During that time, Dolly Harper and Jon Testman nailed Mary's lamb. Spot on. Not a mistake.

"And now." My teacher rose and yawned. "May I introduce Coraline Raine, playing 'Mary Had a Little Lamb.'"

Obligatory clapping began, and I glanced at my parents. Mom pursed her lips, Dad smiled, and I slid off the end of the pew, marched toward the Steinway.

"Dead girl walking!"

No, I didn't actually hear that, but I felt it and every gaze that bored a hole in my back. I reached the piano, plopped onto the bench, and tried to breath.

Start. Start.

My legs swung so hard they kicked the piano.

"Crow!" Mom hissed from the audience. "Sit still and play."

I peeked around the big hall. I peeked at my piano teacher, shifting in her seat. I peeked at Mom, and her clenched teeth, and her closed eyes. Finally, I peeked at Dad, at his gentle face. I lifted my hands, placed them on the keys, and played.

Seven notes.

Blank. I went blank. As my last note faded into silence,

I started to rock. My eyes stung, and I started again.

"Mary Had a Little Lamb . . ."

I slowly bowed my head and closed my eyes. I couldn't move. I was dying in front of everyone. And it was no small death.

Then: arms. They rounded my shoulder. I opened my eyes as Dad played a lovely introduction to my song. He paused and whispered, "I hate recitals. Will you play with me?"

I relaxed, and together we played it right through. No mistakes. The crowd thundered in applause.

"I love you, Dad."

"I love you, too."

He left us the next morning.

—

I stared out that bus window, at Shane's faint reflection. It was true, my classmates wanted to see Jasmine dead, but they didn't know Death like I did. It's one thing to get all excited about it in the abstract. Quite another to see it real. There's a hideous silence to Death. It's not loud, or video-game exciting. It's quiet and weighty, and it steals your words.

Like the silence immediately following a car crash. Like the silence of a botched piano recital.

Sarcastic laughter floated back from the girls in front of me, and I slumped in my seat. Not two days into my walkabout, and already I had added attempted murder to Crow's world. Not exactly my goal.

"Is this seat taken?"

I peeked up at Addy.

"No. Please, sit."

She eased herself down. "I saw you get off with Crow this morning."

"Yeah."

"I haven't seen you before." Her eyes were large and welcoming.

I'd been waiting so long for this chance, and now, alone with Addy, I had nothing to say.

"You know," Addy said, "she's really great."

"Who?"

"Crow." Addy folded her hands. "My teacher told me what happened today, and, well, I just don't want you to get freaked out about it. She's such a great sister; she's my sister, you know. And she doesn't have too many friends. I'd hate to see her lose one she just met."

I blinked, unbelieving. Adele was watching out for me. My mind whirred. How many other times had she secretly covered my back?

"She won't lose me."

Addy leaned back. "That's good. Really good."

I didn't see Crow the next day. I knew she wouldn't spend her nights in the tree house, not with the Monster back home to worry about, but I thought she'd come out during the day. No, not to thank me, she'd never do that, but maybe to rip me for interference.

By the second morning of Crow's suspension, she still had not shown her face, and I was hungry. I tramped off to school to eat lunch. It was easy enough. The rear gym door was always open, and once sardined among two thousand kids, it was unlikely that I'd be noticed.

"Hey, Shane!"

Maybe not so unlikely.

Basil stood three kids behind me in the pizza line. "Sit with us?"

"Us?"

"Me and Scoot and Mel."

I shrugged and held out my tray. "Yeah, that's fine." I turned toward the lunch lady seated behind the scanner.

She held out her hand, waiting for my card. When I didn't offer one, she glanced up and I winced. "Shane Owen. I forgot—"

"Out of credits, dear? Let's check." She punched on her computer. "You never had any. Consider this your last reminder."

"Here," Basil pushed forward and swiped his twice. "She's good."

There was something genuinely odd about the gesture. I never noticed it the first time around, and he paid for plenty of my meals. It was the sense of obligation I felt after he did it, as if I owed him something. That was true. Basil kept score of kindnesses and would one day demand a repayment, which would cost me everything. But I'm getting ahead of myself.

I followed Basil to our table. It wasn't really ours: time and repetition had simply staked our claim. Mel glanced up at me with passing disgust, quickly followed by the smile that stretched a mile wide and a millimeter deep.

"Shane." She glanced at Basil. "How did you find her?"

"Pizza line."

"Just like Crow." She poked around her low-fat salad with low-fat dressing. "She really reminds me of her."

"You don't know anything." Scoot shoveled in a scoop of mashed potatoes and kept talking, white potatoes clinging to the corners of his lips. "Shane ends fights. Crow starts 'em."

Scoot and Mel rehashed the story, while Basil stared at me. It was a strange look, a cross between affection and amusement. He always tried to get in people's heads.

"What?" I put down my fork and glared.

"Just looking, is all." He reached for his pizza, but his gaze never left me. "How's Crow?"

Mel quieted, and from the corner of my eye, I saw her turn.

"I don't know. I haven't talked to her since."

Basil chewed his lip and stretched out his hand, placed it on the lunch table palm up.

I don't know what it was about Basil. He was easy enough on the eyes, but you'd never find him in a magazine, and he certainly wasn't the best athlete in town. More likely it was the secrets; his disarming grin always extracted a bit more information than I wanted to share. Yet something in his gaze convinced me that my feelings were safe with him. Then there was his confidence. He had a certainty about him. Basil's suggestions, no matter how ludicrous, just felt right. If you know anyone like that, you'll understand why seconds later I found myself holding his hand. And a few seconds after that, I was wearing Mel's salad.

Mel marched out of the lunchroom, and I scowled and picked lettuce leaves from my hair. "Thanks for lunch, Basil, and give my thanks to Mel for the extra serving. I, uh, need to go find Crow."

"Let me go with you," he said. "I haven't skipped in ages."

"No!" I stumbled away from the table. "No, I'll be fine."

Basil jumped up and walked toward me. "But you don't know where she is." He reached out and gently removed a piece of romaine from my shoulder.

I paused. "And you do."

"Yeah, I do."

I grabbed a napkin and swiped low-fat ranch dressing from my forehead. "Show me."

Basil and I slipped out of the mayhem, crept downstairs to the gym door, and raced across the field.

"Just tell me where she is." I huffed, and doubled over.

He slowed and walked back toward me. "She's with my mom."

Of course!

I straightened and jogged away from Basil. In his middle school form, he was officially a pest whose presence hindered my work. And my work was to find Crow, to stay with her, to help her change the course of one day. It was possible; I'd seen events change with Jasmine and, with them, Crow's future.

Together, we could protect Addy. Yes, Sadie wanted me to focus on my life, but she probably wasn't briefed on my sister's fate.

I reached the bus stop just as the Metro ground to a stop.

"Hold up! You'll never find her!" Basil pounded behind me.

Wrong.

I couldn't forget. There was one adult who made me think growing up might be worth the effort: Basil's mom— hippy throwback, Save Tibet activist. I believed it rare that a cop would end up hitched to the woman who, upon their first meeting at a PETA rally, smacked him in the nose. But he arrested her, cuffed her, brought her in . . . and fell in love. Such were Officer David and Dove Dewey, Basil's odd-couple parents.

I shook thoughts of Dove from my mind and climbed bus steps, Basil screaming in the background. I slotted my coins and plunked down, trying to recall when I first met Dove. The time escaped me. The location did not.

Officer Dewey purchased a plot of land outside city limits. He claimed he wanted a place for target practice, but the truth was that Dove had demanded a garden Basil's apartment complex couldn't provide. A cop's pay didn't allow for a house, so Dewey dropped an old RV right in the center of the land, considering it both a great place to store his guns and a first-rate poker getaway.

I don't imagine he figured on Dove's moving out and taking up residence.

"Oh, I still love the man," she used to say. "It's the living with him I can't stomach."

She claimed the RV, turned the plot of land into gardens, and Officer Dewey never got in even one hand of poker.

The RV became Basil's second home, and eventually Crow's sanctuary.

What a tangled web Basil and I did weave.

⌣

Basil's hand jammed the accordion bus doors, and he staggered up, collapsing next to me in the front seat. I chuckled and turned away, again letting my head *thunk* against the window. Shane must've done that often, as it felt so natural.

"See, Crow and my mom have always had this thing," Basil said.

"Yes, they did. I know about your family. I know Dove and the officer."

He frowned. "Crow tells you more than most. So tell me about yours." He nudged my shoulder. "Your and Crow's dad. Where's he at now?"

"Kentucky."

"Kentucky." Basil rolled his eyes. "Great accent."

"Well, first Alaska, and then recently Kentucky."

Basil held up his hand. "Okay, dead." It was a possibility, and it both ended all the family talk and provided a nice reason for my sudden appearance at Crow's tree house.

The bus bounced on, slow and hypnotic. A stray leaf of romaine lettuce fell from my hair. I peeked at Basil, so comfortable in this crazy world of mine.

"Hey, Basil, why do you put up with Mel?" I lowered my voice. "And what do you see in Crow?"

The instant the words were out, I wished I could reel them back.

Please, don't make a joke about this.

To Basil's credit, he did not. He straightened, bit his lip, and nodded.

"Fair questions. Mel is a wind, nothing more, you know? Light, breezy. She never takes you anywhere you don't want to go. She's a head case, but a predictable one. End of story." Basil paused, then whispered Crow's name. "Remember the twister that blew through last year? Probably not, you were in Alaska." He rolled his eyes. "Sky here turned green and the air hung, thick and heavy, waiting. The world was still, birds muted. There was a moment before the winds, an eye of the storm. That's Crow. That heavy place where every word is important and everything she does is symbolic and you're always a moment from a tornado. That's life with Crow." He peeked at me. "I couldn't live without her, but—and no offense to your sister—sometimes the drama gets so heavy you need a light breeze, you know? Just a day at the beach. Enter Mel."

I wondered at the deepest words he'd ever spoken. "Ever told Crow that?"

He frowned and eased back in the seat. "No. I guess I haven't."

We rode the rest of the way in silence. I hopped off at the Park-n-Ride in Maple Grove and trudged toward Elm Creek. Though Basil's words were still with me, he followed a few steps behind. The walk to Dove's took four thousand and three steps, just over an hour. I'd always been into counting, a little obsessive/compulsive tendency that must have slid down Mom's DNA strand into my own mind, and apparently my soul's.

Basil caught up to me.

"You do know where you're going."

I paused. No talk. It cluttered up my thinking. "Yeah. Three thousand five hundred steps that way." I pointed.

He bit his lip and shook his head. "You're a little more like Crow than I thought."

I can't explain the feeling I had with Basil at my side and Dove minutes away. The whole going-back thing, you'd think, would be déjà vu at every turn. But it wasn't. I mean, this wasn't. I'd lived to eighteen. My life had filled with five more years of strange twists and vivid memories, and in this young body I felt oddly detached.

I was a visitor.

Until I reached Dove's plot.

Her lot bordered Elm Creek on the back, shielded on either side by pine trees both tall and full. The grass was wild, just like Dove. Gardens filled the back half of the acreage. "After all," she said, "I should leave some land for David."

Later on, those gardens would take over the entire property.

I stepped into the tall grass and ran my fingers over its gentle wave. Maybe this is where the field in Lifeless's dream was born. Dove worked the flower bed and slowly stood as Basil and I approached.

"Dove. It's been so long," I said, and broke into a broad smile.

She leaned hard on her hoe. "Do I know you?"

"Well, I've heard so much from Crow, I feel like I know you already."

"That's a pile of crap." She bent over and worked more dirt. "I don't know who you're talking about." She looked up. "Nice of you to come, Basil. School treating you well?"

"Day in, day out. You know." Basil stepped forward. "Ma, this is Crow's half sister. She needs to find her."

Dove paused. "Half sister. Where you from, half sister?"

I peeked at Basil, couldn't recall what I'd told him. "Wisconsin?"

"Now I know she's full of crap." Dove turned her back.

Basil walked toward her and whispered in her ear. She peeked over her shoulder and breathed deep. "I'll be right back."

Dove disappeared into the trailer. From the beginning, she was my protector. I never witnessed this until I came as Shane, but I always felt it to be true. She wouldn't let anybody near me. I loved her so.

Dove poked her head out the door. "Come on in, Basil, Shane. Don't make too much noise."

We followed her into the trailer. Inside, it was dark, not a light on, and we stumbled toward the back bedroom.

"Crow?" Basil called. "It's me. You back here?"

"Yeah, I want to see Shane."

Crow's outline sat on the bed cross-legged. I pushed in front of Basil, toward the smell of cigarette smoke and alcohol, and sat on the foot of the bed.

"Good to see ya, Shane, you little witch."

"Keep talking," I said.

There was silence here, and finally I turned to Basil. "You can go."

Basil shifted. "It's my mom's place. I've known Crow a lot longer than—"

"You can go, Basil." Crow said quietly.

He tongued his cheek and backed out. "Yeah, right. I'll be with Mom if you need me."

Our shadows looked at each other for five minutes. "So,

how are you getting along? Do you need anything?" I asked.

"Why didn't you let me kill her?"

Kill her? Oh, Jasmine.

"I appreciate how enjoyable that would have been for you, but I'm telling you that in the long run, murder's more a negative than a positive."

Her voice quieted. "Maybe. What time is it?"

"Six or so."

"I need to get home."

"I know." I shifted on the bed. "Why'd you do it? Why push Jasmine through?"

Crow gave a heavy sigh. "She called me a psycho bitch, and I held it together. But then she called you one, too."

"There was no more?" I asked. "That's it?"

She hung her head. "Nobody says anything about my sister, real or you."

I scooted up next to Crow. "I'm gonna turn on the lamp. Close your eyes."

Click.

"Holy . . ."

Crow's skin was ashen, her cheeks drawn. She sat amid beer cans and cigarette boxes and books. She winced and slowly opened her eyelids. Crow had no whites, only reds.

I reached over and hugged her, felt her collapse against my side.

"Shane, Jasmine said your name, but inside I heard

Adele's. I looked at her face, but I saw Jude's. I couldn't help it. I lost it."

I know. You'll always protect Adele.

———

It was my first memory and, oddly, one of my most potent.

A Dad memory. It should have been precious.

Mom worked late at the library, while the two of us struggled to get Adele into bed. A number of obstacles stood in the way, the largest being "the tub": a soapy, drippy experience that left all three of us soaked.

"Run the water, Coraline." Dad frowned at Adele's diaper. "I'll go to work on the back end."

I jumped to the tub and soon had it filled with foam. "Ready, Daddy!"

He nodded. "Okay, here we go. One. Two . . ." He yanked off the diaper. "Three!" He hoisted her off the counter and plunged her deep into the water.

For a second all was quiet.

Then little Addy wailed.

"It's all right, darlin'. Just a bath."

She arched her back and screamed. Dad repositioned her and swore. "That water is scalding hot!" He drew Addy out, her skin mottled and red, and wrapped her loosely in a towel. "To the car, Coraline! We need to take her in."

I remember little about that urgent-care visit, except for

the fish tank. I plastered my face against the glass and cried.

Addy's skin eventually returned to a proper shade, so the episode turned out well.

Until Mom came home, heard the story, and flew into a rage. Dad slept on the couch that night. I know, because I snuggled with him.

"I can't do this, Cor," I remember his whisper, as well as my toddler resolve.

After that, I made a promise to myself. *I will never let Addy get hurt again.*

"You know," Crow rasped. "You said you watched my silhouette through the window? That's true. I pace to stay awake. If I sleep and he comes . . ."

"You don't need to tell me."

"But I do; I've got to tell someone. If I sleep, and Jude slips in . . . I don't trust him. He wants to do a lot more than touch her, I just know it. I've told Mom again and again . . . how he looks at Addy, what I've heard in the hallway. She doesn't believe me. Since Dad left, she believes nothing I say. But Mom's not dumb. She sees it, and I see the knowing in her face, but Jude's got her all tangled up in his psycho-babble. He says Addy needs a strong male in her life. He says I'm bitter and trying to turn the family against him, and Mom buys it because she wants to, she needs to. She buys it all and ignores it all and there's not one person in this damn world who believes me." Crow's body shook. "I keep it from Addy 'cause I don't want to scare her, but you, you've *got* to believe me."

"I do." I rocked her gently and stroked her hair. "I so believe you, and you need to believe me. Nothing's going to happen to Addy. We can stop him. . . . I promise you: we can do it."

Crow squeezed tighter and I squeezed back, and it felt so good to hug myself. I never let anyone get this close at thirteen, but she just let me in. Way in. Crow was changing, softening. And that might be good.

Except that hardness alone kept me sane.

"Last time you ate?" I asked.

"Two days ago."

Inside, I boiled. This woman who gave me shelter cared little about my life. Were all mothers like that? "Dove's just letting you die back here!"

Crow straightened. "No. She's letting me live. My way." She rose from the bed. "Gotta get home. The Monster will be home soon."

"I'll go with you."

Crow pushed by me, wobbled, and regained her balance. She reached back and squeezed my arm. "You should have let me kill her."

I shook my head and grinned. "With a trophy? Where's the glamour in that?"

Crow chuckled and marched toward the door, paused but did not turn. "Don't leave me, Shane."

"I'm not going anywhere."

"I'd ask you to sleep over tonight if I didn't live with him."

"I'm not afraid."

Crow spun around, her lips curled. "All right. But I'll tell you right now, I don't sleep much."

"I know. We'll watch together."

Side by side, we pushed out into the last rays of sunlight. One week till Mayday. One week to change Addy's world. *Soon Crow, I'll need you, too.*

CHAPTER 8

THE THOUGHTS OF C. RAINE

Home is where one starts from.
T. S. Eliot

CAN YOU LIKE YOURSELF MORE WHEN YOU AREN'T YOURSELF?

I only know that we stepped into Mom's house at eight o'clock, and I had an admiration for Crow—for me—that I'd never before experienced. I was proud of her, which I guess meant I was proud of me. I had to admit, for a girl who defined life in terms of degrees of failure, it felt good.

Awkward.

"Follow me." Crow walked into the kitchen and stopped. She spun and hustled me out, but a voice didn't let us get far.

"Look who dragged in!" Jude the Monster rose from the table and took a step forward. "You look half dead, Crow. Get some sleep tonight, will you?" His eyes roamed me, finally settling on my face. "And what's your name, young lady?" He held out his hand.

"I'm not a lady. I'm a girl. Then again, I'm told you're not much of a man, so let's just skip the intro part." I turned to Crow, her red eyes wide with shock. "Is your mom or Adele around? I'd like to meet them."

Jude dropped his hand and cursed. "Another Crow."

I shrugged. "I'll take that as a compliment."

Crow rounded my shoulder with her arm, pulled me through the kitchen and down the hall. "That may have been the single best moment I've experienced in thirteen years of life."

"Glad to provide it for you."

"Mom?" Crow called. "Mom!"

"We're in here." Adele called from the bedroom.

My heartbeat quickened, and Crow opened the door, collapsed on her bed. "I'm really hungry. Any leftovers?"

"Where were you?" Mom didn't turn. "Dove's, I assumed."

They say that when you die, your whole life passes before your eyes. I didn't believe that, especially given that I had some experience in the matter. But as I stood, my gaze again fixed on Addy, the one I'd come back to save, and yeah, the dam broke and the memories flooded.

I saw her take her first steps. I did, not Mom or Dad. Me.

I caught her when she fell off the monkey bars. Well, I broke her fall a little.

I taught her to ride her bike.

So many successes. One failure overshadowed them all.

"My fault," I said, and jarred my gaze free of Adele. "I was showing Crow where I lived."

Mom whipped around. "Which is . . . ?"

"Alabama."

Mom's face twitched. "I'm guessing you're Shane Owen Raine."

"That's what they're calling me. I admit the last name was borrowed without permission."

I tried hard to stay callous, detached. But the whole scene was too much: Mom barking at me; Addy leaning against the bedpost, her knees tucked up beneath her chin; and Crow collapsed on a bed, looking very similar to the crooked soul I'd seen in the hospital.

I wanted to scream, It's me. I'm back! I'm Crow's soul-mind, whatever that is. Do you have any idea what's going to happen in just a few days?

Instead, I eased onto Crow's bed and glanced around at everything that once had been mine. "It's nice to meet you, Ms. Raine."

"Yeah." Mom said, nodding slowly. "Seeing as how you live here, it's nice to finally get a look at your face." She glanced at Crow. "Meat loaf in the fridge."

Crow looked at her hard. "The Monster's in there, too."

Mom wiped her brow with her middle finger. "That

monster is my husband, a fact I hoped you would have accepted by now."

Crow shook her head.

"What?" Mom raised her eyebrows. "No comeback? No sick, perverted accusations against him? Shane, you're already having a positive effect." She glanced at the three of us. "I need to consult with Jude." Mom kissed Adele and left the room.

A strange silence settled over us. Adele, immune to the gravity of such moments, found her voice first.

"The girl from the bus. So you're the one Crow's told me about these last nights. You've really been living in our backyard?"

I peeked out the window. "Yeah, I hope that's okay."

She grinned. So gentle, so at ease with whatever came into her life. Adele plopped down next to Crow and stroked her hair. Crow slowly closed her eyes. "Thanks for anything you did for my sister." She paused. "I'm sorry for Mom. She's having a rough day."

Crow shot up to vertical, red eyes wide. "It's more than a day. We can pretend later, but I'm not lying to Shane: this is every morning, this is every night, this is her."

Addy lowered her head and folded her hands.

"And I'm getting it. I'm getting it all, you know that," Crow continued. "But you know how half of this is Jude speaking through her. He puts on that therapist face and pretty much convinces her the sky is green. He's taking over the house, Addy."

Addy peeked up and whispered, "I don't want to talk about this again."

Crow glanced at the door and lowered her voice. "But we have to. Jude isn't right."

"He's friendly enough."

"To you. Do you notice? Only to you. Touchy, waiting, watching."

Addy rubbed her arms, "I don't know what you're saying."

"Why did Dad leave? I know I made it tough. I get that, so I'm not innocent." Crow peeked at me, her face softening. "But I've been thinking lately: there must have been another reason. That reason is Jude."

Keep talking, Crow.

"Dad's probably happy, wherever he is. Adele, we don't have to stay either. You and I could—"

"I'm not leaving Mom. She needs us. I need her."

How many times I'd danced around the issue: *Run away with me! We could do it.* Each time it came back to the same thing. This curious, unreasonable connection between Adele and Mom. Though Mom was little more than an extension of Jude, Addy would not let her go.

The sisters fell silent.

"The main thing is that you two stay together," I said. "And more than together, trust each other, trust that you have each other's best interests in mind." They glanced at me, and at each other. Then they hugged.

I should have been a therapist.

"So you're the daughter of my ex-husband." Mom strutted in. "Given your age, my ex would have likely rushed from Regions Hospital, where I had Crow, to the bedside of his mistress, who would have been busy producing you." She paused. "Then again, Crow's entrance into the world would make almost any man do that."

Her face darkened, the face that blamed Crow for Dad's departure. "Yes, Crow would make any man hungry for a different home."

"No, Mom," Addy grabbed Crow's wrist. "You need to stop saying that. He loved us both."

Crow stormed out of the room, and my gaze followed. Those digs had been so common, so everyday; I never felt their cruelty, not from the inside. But now, I saw the sickness of the words, the disease that spread through the house.

"Maybe Dad was a polygamist," I said. "Or a sperm donor. Or maybe you just forgot that you had a third child, ever thought of that?"

Adele burst out laughing, and the dark shadow passed from Mom's face. She chuckled. "I declare, you are something." Her eyes narrowed. "You are something. You know, you do look like Cameron. It's in the eyes." She sighed.

"So the school wanted to know if I claimed you. I told them that depended on whether you tilted toward Crow or Adele."

"Two fine choices, if you ask me. What do you think?" I asked.

"Time will tell. I don't know where you rightfully belong, so I won't sign anything legal, but if you can keep Crow on the straight and narrow, you can stay here for life."

Straight and narrow. I hated those words, and they kicked me into a memory.

Confession time. Aside from my little thirteen-year-old flirtation with an empty garage and Jude's Winstons, the only place I ever drank or smoked was at Dove's. I did no other drug, and committed no crime other than those against my own body. I couldn't afford to—I had to be coherent for the nights.

Despite my reasonably responsible attitude toward substance abuse, I found myself in juvenile detention four times, four of the most terrifying nights of my life. I was never there for more than a night, and never for an instant was I frightened for myself. Though Jude's nighttime visits to our room had long since ended, fear for Addy's safety died hard, if at all.

I was sixteen when I had my first juvie sleepover. The

night had started innocently enough. Basil came over to the house and picked me up on his new pea-green snowmobile. Proud fool. I threw on my leather jacket and ran out the door. Mom called, "Basil, now keep that daughter of mine on the straight and narrow."

This frustrated me for two reasons:

- Mom was acting like a mom. There's a joke.

- Had Mom ever seen the inside of Basil's room, she'd have discovered a boatload of dubiously acquired electronic devices. I will not say he was a thief. Thieves actually believe they are taking someone else's property. Basil simply possessed an entitlement mentality—he felt entitled to Jack Logan's iPad and Mr. Scapelli's laptop.

"Sure thing," Basil answered. He smiled and messed my hair. "Crow on the straight and narrow. You can trust me."

We ended up at the Shack, home of the most incredible pizza pies. If I remember correctly, Basil ended up with a hot pepper fleck lodged in his eye, which swelled to the size of a golf ball. He whimpered and whined until I demanded he take me home.

We sat and talked on his sled in my driveway. That's when I noticed it, the bungee basket, not exactly standard equipment for a new snowmobile. I lifted the lid. Five cans of spray paint.

Basil offered a sheepish smile. "I thought maybe—"

"What maybe were you thinking?"

"Why let jocks have all the fun?" He climbed off the sled, removed a can of paint, and shook. "Big game tonight. I thought we could head over to East High and show some school spirit. I always thought you and I should paint this town."

"Have a nice night, Basil."

I slid off his machine and took one step.

"Hey, Crow."

I turned. I should never have turned, but I did, and Basil released a blast of paint that speckled my hair, my coat, my shoes.

"Jerk!"

I stumbled through the front door at exactly nine o'clock, an important detail here, and tripped over a pile of Mom's junk. I reached the bedroom and vented to Addy, who spent the rest of the evening removing all hint of yellow from my hair. The next morning, a Saturday, not five minutes after Addy left for basketball practice, Principal Hawkins and Basil's dad showed up on my doorstep with "evidence" that I had defaced archrival East High School. Apparently, the letters *C R* had been sprayed all over their school in bright yellow paint.

"It wasn't smart, Crow. I could overlook you defacing

their field house, but the school itself?" Officer Dewey shook his head. "Signing your initials doesn't show much remorse. Not smart."

"What's not smart is your thinking I'd do that. Have you spoken to Basil about last night?"

Dewey cleared his throat. "I took that liberty, Crow. According to my son, he had you back here by nine. Where you went after that is, sadly, a bit unclear."

"Unclear?" Principal Hawkins stepped into the house. I pointed to his foot.

"Can he do that? Legally, can he do that?"

Dewey gentled out the steaming principal and asked for my mom. I explained to all of them that I was in my bedroom out of habit, one formed from spending my childhood protecting my sister from a psychotic stepdad bent on sexual abuse.

Mom offered a nervous laugh. She much preferred the principal's rendition of the previous evening.

"Crow, I'm sorry, but it's the right thing to do." She opened the closet and removed my leather coat, speckled with Basil's stupidity. Mom assumed her most pained look. "No parent likes to see her daughter in trouble."

It did not matter to them that *C R* also stood for Central Rules, or that yellow was our school's color. Nor did it matter that sportos *always* spray-painted after said contest.

My jacket flecked yellow.

I had signed my handiwork.

They found their culprit.

Case closed.

The cost of covering for my friend was steep. Mom let me sit in juvie for the remainder of the day and throughout the night, I believe as much for my attempted whistle-blowing as any perceived misdeeds. Sunday morning she skipped church to pay me a visit.

We stared at each other on a television monitor, the phone crackling and whistling. "When are you going to stop?" she asked. "What exactly does 'straight and narrow' mean to you?"

"Death, or killing Basil, whichever comes first."

Mom's jaw tightened.

"Wrong answer?" I looked away, and then stared her straight in the eye. "'Straight and narrow'? How about marrying a guy who prefers you over your daughter?"

Click.

I slowly hung up. I'd never said it so clearly, and the playback made me wince. It would be two more months until Mom next spoke to me.

I shook my head back into the present, or the past. Whatever.

Adele jumped up. "Oh, I really like her. Can she sleep in here?"

Here, Mom's face lost its mirth. It seemed clear that a piece of her knew this room wasn't safe for a girl.

Adele shrugged. "Or you can put her in the guest room—"

"No!" Mom said, anxiety getting the best of her face. "Best not sleep there alone. I mean, what's the fun in that? Crow's in here. This is where you can spend the night. Shane, I do need to know where you belong. I'm not like Dove. Do I need to call Alabama?" Her face softened, coming as near to concern as I'd ever seen it venture. "Isn't someone, somewhere, going to miss you tonight?"

I shook my head. "I'm unclaimed."

Mom tightened her lips, and Adele ran over and hugged me. "I claim you!" Firm and trusting and Adele: I felt it, I felt her. How long I'd waited for her embrace. It was all worth it.

She ran into the hall and quickly returned with Crow.

"What did you say to Mom?" Crow asked.

"I told her your dad was a polygamist."

Crow cocked her head. "You know just what to say. To everyone."

The cuckoo clock struck nine. Both Crow and I looked at Adele, spoke in unison, "Get in bed, Addy. You're safe tonight."

Crow shot me a horrified look.

I winced. "That was weird, wasn't it?"

"Sure. Weird." Crow shoved her bed in front of the door and grabbed a compilation of Greek myths. She hopped onto the comforter and started to read. I grabbed the *Iliad* and joined her, leaning against her footboard. A few minutes into Homer, I set down the book.

"I'll take a shift, Crow. Get some rest. You look, well, awful."

Crow gazed longingly at her pillow, then flew to the bottom of the bed and grabbed my collar. "Do you know what I'll do to you if you let me down, if you fall asleep?"

I gently grabbed her wrist, and she let go. "You're safe tonight, Crow." I glanced at Adele, so at peace, already drifted into a safer place. "Give it to me."

Crow bit her lip, leaned back, reached beneath the mattress, and removed the butcher knife. She lay it carefully between my outstretched legs and snuggled down. A minute later, Crow slept. It was fitful and shallow, but it was sleep. Maybe enough to turn her eyes from red to pink.

The urge came to turn out the light. At least the ceiling light. The lamps would be enough to keep me awake. But I watched Crow toss, desperate to rejoin Adele, and realized her belief in me was complete. No, every light would stay on. I would take no chances.

I stared up and counted lumps on the textured ceiling. My mind relaxed. Jude would risk nothing tonight, not with a guest over.

I reached 8,276, and wind rattled the window. The night was calm and the orphan breeze departed, but its sound, like gentle breathing, remained. I eased myself up and pressed my ear to the door. A shuffle, and then all was still—Jude motionless, but not breathless. I swung my feet off the bed, and Crow's eyes shot open. Her eyebrows raised, and I pointed at the knob. I reached for a pad of paper and a pen, scribbled a note, and handed it to Crow. She mouthed the words—*We won't let you touch her, Monster*—looked at me, and grinned. Carefully, she slid under her bed and slipped the note beneath the door. It quickly vanished.

Footsteps thudded away down the hall.

Crow crawled back onto the bed. I looked at her, and she stared at Adele.

"Shane, what do you think of when you look at me? I mean, nobody else lives like this. Am I crazy?"

I closed my eyes and shook my head. When next I opened them, Crow fiddled with a locket suspended from a chain around her neck. A locket I knew well.

"My dad was a writer." She pointed over her shoulder at her "shelf of great minds," which was bulging with philosophy books. "He bought me all those; I guess he thought I'd read them someday."

"Was he right?"

Crow gazed at her hands. "There's one I read a lot. My dad wrote it. I write, too, did I tell you that? It's all I've ever wanted to do. Write, like Dad."

I felt a tear forming and squinted it back. "So why don't you?"

Crow looked over at Adele, then down to her locket. "I'm so tired. The ideas come, they go, and I can hardly hold them in my head. But the real reason?" She sighed. "Dad came into the room. I pretended to be asleep. He kissed Addy. He kissed me. 'My Coraline, look after Addy when I'm gone.' That's what he said." Crow paused. "So at five, my life was already planned. Dad gave me a job, and it wasn't to write, and I vowed I wouldn't fail him. So far I haven't."

She tucked the locket back in her pajamas.

"Do you know how much Adele looks up to me? I'm her hero. She's nearly perfect and I'm such a nothing, but I'm her hero. Why is that?"

"Because a minute ago, when you slipped Jude that note, you *were* a hero."

Crow puffed out air and stared at her sister. "You aren't going to stay with us long, are you?"

"I don't know," I said quietly. "Why?"

She curled up and flung her Greek myth compilation at my chest. Crow's body seemed smaller, and her words shook. "Read the book: All the good people go. Only monsters remain."

CHAPTER 9

THE THOUGHTS OF C. RAINE

C'est une chose anormale de vivre. Living is abnormal.
Eugène Ionesco

I WOKE THE NEXT MORNING with an anxious chord pounding in my stomach. I rose from the bed and peeked in the mirror. Still Shane. Addy rolled over and drew her blankets over her shoulders. Safe there. I grabbed my balled-up jeans from the day before and dug out my locket. The vibrant green was gone, replaced by a dull pastel glow. Something was changing. Time was passing.

No matter, I'm just days away from changing everything.

Crow looked a little better—that being, of course, in measures of small degree. Three years of sleep deprivation is not cured in a night, and that's what she carried.

A word about her ritual, which was my ritual, and the night it started.

I was ten, and still trying to make sense of Dad's departure. Mom's blame was hard to dispute. Their final night's argument had raged throughout the house and was punctuated with plenty of "Crow."

Jude the Monster was well entrenched in our home by then. He had first turned his perverted eye in Mom's direction when she and Dad went to consult with him in his role as family therapist/marriage counselor. I recall Mom returning from those sessions with a certain glow, strange to a child, but certainly noticeable. Dad came home equally affected, though in a dour direction. Soon Dad was gone, Dr. Jude had filled his shoes, and we assumed the shape of the typical American family.

Until, I think, Jude's midnight tuck-ins. At first, tender enough. A straightening of the sheets, a sweet "good night," a quick wink.

It was a Thursday, and around midnight. Why I lay awake, I do not know, but as the door swung open, I did the natural thing for any child: I feigned unconsciousness. Jude walked over and pulled the sheets off Adele. He stood for minutes, staring. His face and hands twitched; something evil wanted to be unleashed.

He bent over and kissed her, then reached his hand toward her pajama bottoms. . . .

And I screamed and leaped out of bed. I kept right on screaming.

Would you believe Jude straightened, shook his head, and pulled his hair? "What am I doing?" He uttered tormented curses and ran from the room.

He stole nothing from Adele that night, but though I had no words for it at the time, I felt something dying inside of me. The Monster took my childhood.

His trips to our bedroom became more frequent. Always, he moved toward Adele. Always, I screamed until Mom's footsteps *thumped* down the steps or Jude cursed and left the room. Blocking the door with the bed came later, as did my late-night-"sandwich" knife, which accompanied my full understanding of the Monster's intent.

How can you doubt Mom's knowledge at some level? How can you wake to a missing man night after night? Here, I learned the power of belief, and denial. The truth would have killed her, so she refused to see it.

Couple that with the twisted tongue of a trusted therapist—one able to reframe suspicious actions in a reasonable light—and yeah, I suppose it explained Mom's lack of action.

Jude's lies never worked on me. He swore me to silence about his "friendly" visits, a vow I would break only once to Officer Dewey. It was a calculated concession on my part. I could protect Addy at night, but I couldn't follow her all day. Jude's certain and horrid threats against my sister guaranteed that if I told anyone about his "concerns," I would not see Addy again. Looking back it seems a stretch, but blinded by affection for the one I cherished, I could not take the chance.

You're never so vulnerable as when you're in love.

———

I walked into the kitchen. If you didn't know better, the family appeared a contented lot. Mom worked the stove, producing a fine set of pancakes. Crow and Adele plunked down and ate quickly, though one more vigorously than the other. Jude sipped coffee and read the paper.

"Famine in Ethiopia reaches new depths." Jude sighed. "Those poor people. How fortunate we are to have this food, this family."

"Hey, Shane." Crow gagged, then gestured with her fork toward the bench in the corner. "Pull on up."

I walked to the cupboard and grabbed a plate, reached over to the drawer by the fridge and claimed a fork, then swiped a napkin from the bin behind the toaster.

I pulled up to the table. All eyes were on me.

"I declare." Mom's hands rose to her hips. "You move around this kitchen like you've lived here your whole life."

I bit my lip. "Oh, yeah, it's set up so logically."

Jude cleared his throat and rattled the paper. "Big storm

coming tonight. You'll all want to dress warm and be in early."

His swipes at compassion left a lump in my throat. How could a man care about the dying, go to work, save some marriages, destroy others, return home, and destroy his stepchildren? How can all that exist within one man? What do you say to that? As Crow, I never had an answer.

But Shane did.

"Did you get my note, Jude?"

He slowly lowered the paper and shot a quick glance at Mom, busy clanking dishes.

"I don't know what note that would be, Shane." His eyes widened and then narrowed.

"The one I slipped under the door last night. The one I gave to the heavy breather standing in the hallway outside Adele's room."

Mom's clanking stopped, but she did not turn.

Have you seen rage cross a face? Disfigure it? Change it? That evil I mentioned took him over, and my heart beat irregularly. Crow glanced down. Only Adele ate on, a slow, thoughtful act. This topic had never before reached the kitchen.

"Why were you in the hall, Jude?" Crow's jaw was tight. "I'm curious what you were doing out there."

"Crow! Don't talk to Jude like that." Mom's voice quieted. "There's always a reason."

"Did I speak with a harsh tone?" Crow's hand opened and closed, a storm gathering strength. I remembered Basil's description.

Tornado is coming.

"Is everybody here crazy?" she continued. "It's all right there." She pointed at Jude. "It's a sickness right here in front of our faces, but we cover our eyes and live like insane—"

"Enough!" Mom pounded the sink and spun around. "Enough, enough . . . enough. How much do you want to take from me?"

I stared around the room, at Adele's confusion, at the growing crack in Mom's denial. I peeked at Jude's anger, and finally I faced Crow, me, now standing, in the center of it all. She alone fought for what was left of our family, for the only kernel of hope she could see. The truth.

It would likely cost her dearly—courage in hell usually does—but in her challenge I heard her heart, her care for Addy, her hope for Mom. She was like Dad, verbally abused but in love. Yet she was so much more than him. She was still here, fighting the battle that should have been his.

"What would we lose?" Crow approached Mom, gently grabbed her wrist. "Without him, what would we lose? We'd be okay."

Jude cleared his throat. "How many days will you be with us, Shane?" He folded his paper and smoothed his tie.

I folded my hands. "Do I offend you?"

"No, but you seem to have upset the balance of my home. Balance is everything."

And the psychological crap begins.

"Crow, your mother is right. There is always an explanation, but your accusations don't deserve one. How long has it been? And you still live out the shame of your actions as a little child. Let this family heal, Crow. My sessions are sacred, but I had many with your father." He stared at Crow. "He confided many things, things for my ears only, but I tell you this for your benefit, as this pattern must stop. Cameron Raine fled this home for one reason, and from what I've heard, that reason was you."

I wish I could have stood between those words and Crow, because they seemed to pierce like an arrow. Addy jumped to her side, and Crow glanced up, wide-eyed, desperate.

"That's not true." Addy hugged Crow. "It wasn't her fault."

"Oh!" Mom threw up her hands. "Now you've turned Addy against us."

"I'm not against you, Mom; it just can't be right."

Mom and Adele got into it, and Jude looked content. He'd turned the jury on itself.

He reached for his briefcase, removed a sheet of paper from inside, and scrawled a message, his every move calm and deliberate. He pushed the note across the table, and I mouthed the words.

I want to know you better, little pain.

I glanced up and snapped my fingers for a pen. The Monster obliged, reaching across the table and placing one in my outstretched fingers. Passing notes was part of the middle school experience, but here at breakfast with a forty-five-year-old man, the act felt twisted and dirty. I added to his note, balled it up, and tossed it back.

I'm quite certain that before this is over, you will.

He folded it neatly, slipped it into his pocket, and left the room.

Crow and Adele headed for the bedroom, leaving me alone with Mom. Her hands shook, and her voice cracked.

"Shane, you came at a bad time."

"No," I pushed back from the table. "Couldn't be better."

⌣

"How did you do that?"

It had been a quiet walk to the bus stop, but Crow slowed, faced me, and grabbed my shoulders. "Listen, I know you're not normal. Nobody slips in and out of my family without a scratch. You spend time in that house, and you get wounded." She paused. "Angel, demon, ghost—any of those ring a bell?"

I laughed and pulled free. "No. I'm just a girl, Crow. I pay attention."

"Shut up. That sounds like Jude's psycho-babble. You aren't right." She paused. "Do you do dreams?"

"Not following."

"Do you know what they mean? If I told you a dream, could you figure it out?"

I snuck my hand into a pocket and toyed with the locket. "Why do you ask?"

Crow's face fell grim. "The dream came last night." She swallowed. "I was running through a field with Adele. It was all good, you know? Mom was there. I heard Dad, too. Then the Monster showed up."

"What did Mom say?" I asked. "In the field, when it was good. What did she say to you?" I lowered my voice. "I've always wanted to know."

"What are you talking about?" Crow squinted.

"It was all green, right?" I whispered.

"Now you're scaring me. I didn't ask you to tell me my dream, just to interpret. Can you listen without freaking me out?"

"I'm not sure."

Crow stuffed her hands in her pockets, "So yeah, it was all green, until the flowers popped up, yellow everywhere."

"Then—"

"Then I woke. My sheets were drenched, and I had this feeling. I really need to know. I think I was going to die."

I stared into her bloodshot eyes. "Dreams are funny things."

"Am I?"

"You read way too much philosophy at thirteen."

"Am I?"

Sadie said I was a soul-mind, but she said something else, that I couldn't come to awareness until after my physical mind fell asleep, until Crow's mind fell asleep. What if Crow's brain, deep down, knew that truth? What if she dreamed the undertow, rode an unconscious current that told her we both couldn't live at the same time, that one of us would need to go?

Crow knew, even if she didn't know what she knew. As long as I was in her life, there was the real possibility she could not be.

"Shane, I don't care so much for myself, but if I'm not here to be in that room, what happens to Adele?"

"Oh, Crow. There are things I want to tell you." It was my turn to hang my head. "Believe me. Until this threat has disappeared, one of us will always be there with her. Can you just believe me on that?"

Crow stared hard into me. "Okay."

"Good. And get some sleep today."

"Yeah, and you keep going to school. And Shane?" She whisked back her hair. "Whoever you are, stick around."

The bus hissed to a stop, and the first drops of rain fell. Straight-down rain. Rain I knew well. April 30. The door closed, and I took my seat. The sky opened up, and I stared out at Crow statued on the curb. She didn't move until the bus was out of sight.

"What a freak." A girl I'd never seen giggled behind me. "She doesn't even care if she gets all wet."

No, thanks to me, she's got more to worry about.

CHAPTER 10

THE THOUGHTS OF C. RAINE

Hell is empty and all the devils are here.
William Shakespeare

I WALKED INTO SCHOOL THINKING ABOUT THE LAWS OF RETALIATION.
Teens master them. I lived by them. I wondered if, in my
attempt to put Jude in his place, my note had ratcheted up
the stakes for Crow and Adele.

Even in death I was doing damage to myself.

But tonight, all would reverse. I'd make up for everything
I'd done.

My few days back at Midway had seen me transitioned
from regular courses to extended stays in the special
education room. Like Crow, I "struggled" through every
subject, stumbled over every word.

"Now Shane, I *know* you can read this." Ms. Jounquil
placed a few lines before me.

I slowly formed the word. "The bot—"

"Boy."

"The boy and has—"

"His. The word is his."

"The bot and his toy . . ."

Ms. Jounquil threw up her hands. "How is it that a child—"

"Teen."

"How is it that a teen as verbally literate as yourself—"

"You. As literate as you."

"This is pure insanity!" She rose, took a cleansing-breath walk around the room, and plunked down across from Kayla, who by all appearances truly could not read.

"We've reached our last day without Crow." Ms. Hurls, another para with an unfortunate name, pulled up a chair. "It will sure be a lot more interesting when she returns."

I closed my book. I always liked Hurls. She was a no-nonsense, no-trying-to-save-the-world, punch-in/punch-out, type of assistant.

"Did you know"—she chuckled and folded her arms—"that Crow toppled her desk onto my lap the first day she was here?"

Sure do.

I reached for a pencil and doodled on the blank sheet before me. "Do you recall what you said before she did it?"

Ms. Hurls scrunched her face, and then shook her head. "That was a long time ago."

"You said, and I quote, 'Crow, I've heard you were coming. You're Dr. Jude Drayton's daughter. How lucky for you and Adele. To have a man like that work you over? You probably get free personal therapy whenever you need it.'"

She stared at me. "I did say something like that. Crow remembered that? She told you?"

"Yeah, but listen." I set down the pencil and looked her in the eye. "She went home and thought about the whole deal. You couldn't know. She felt bad about the toppling."

"Sure she felt bad." Hurls patted my back, paused, and squinted. "Think she did?"

I sighed. "I know it. According to her, you're one of the good ones here. She told me herself. She told me about everyone. Say, I need a pass to the office."

Hurls, her face aglow, glanced at Ms. Jounquil and slipped me a note. I left the room, clear on what I would do on this, the day before Mayday.

A quick run down the hall brought me to chemistry.

This is going to be painful.

I closed my eyes and pushed into the room. Heads swiveled, and gazes fixed on me.

"Mr. Jenkins?" I stepped in and closed the door behind me. "I come with an apology."

Jenkins didn't bother to glance up. "You come in the middle of a lab. Find me after class and I'll be much more forgiving."

"Normally I would, but there may not be time. This apology is from Crow Raine, who is unable to be here today." A deep hush fell over the room. "Crow is terribly sorry she strapped glass beakers to your chair. Though she did not act alone, she feels bad for her part. The fact that she drew blood makes it worse. It was very unclassy, and she's very sorry."

I felt a loosening deep inside, as if a painful tether had been cut. I felt lighter. No wonder the world dumped their problems on Lifeless.

Mr. Jenkins frowned and removed his spectacles, placing them carefully on the front lab table. "To my knowledge, I will not be blessed with Crow's presence until next year."

"Oops. That's right, that's eighth grade." I backed out of the room. "Just apply that apology to next year and keep your head up, er, rear up, next Halloween, okay?" I slammed the door on a roomful of giggles and headed for phys ed.

If my witness in Lifeless's room did anything, it showed me the healing power of confession. Not the stuck-in-a-box confession to a snoozing priest, but the gut-wrenching kind. Seeking forgiveness runs deeper than words. Forgiveness is supposed to hurt.

It's a fierce act of the will.

I slipped into the girls' bathroom and started a list of my sixth- and seventh-grade sins. As the paper filled, it became harder. My list of major sins stretched beyond fifty, and they involved almost every teacher at Midway. I would omit the kids. I did not have the ream of paper required for those.

I stepped out of the bathroom clear on my goal.

"Shane." Basil leaned against the wall. "Thought I'd find you here."

I peeked at the hall clock. "You just did."

Basil hated closed sentences that left his smooth tongue no room to wriggle.

"And where are you headed now?"

"It's not yours to know. I'm working for Crow."

He crossed his arms and thought a moment. "Then it is my business."

Did you hear that? That not-so-subtle claiming? The result of an entitlement mentality run wild.

"She's too good for you." My words gave me pause. *Is that really true?* "You don't own her, Basil. You'll never own her."

"I don't want to."

I exhaled hard and stormed nearer. "Then what do you want from her? You've been a barnacle on her since you met. You must want something. If you could tell her anything . . . If she was standing right in front of you and you could . . . speak into her soul . . . what would you tell her?"

He winced. "So I'm speaking into her soul? Really weird, Shane, but I'll play along. If she was here I'd, um . . ."

I raised my eyebrows.

"Fine. I'd tell her I don't know what the hell is going on inside her brain or inside her house, and I don't know how to ask about it any clearer. And I don't get why she won't let me in. I mean, does she think I invite Mel to my mom's? She knows everything about my parents, and all I know is that hers treat her like garbage. So I worry. And wipe that look off your face, Shane. I worry 'cause . . .

"'Cause what?"

"'Cause she's special, dammit. There, I said it. I know I don't act like it, but there it is." His breath slowed and evened. "And why I told you that, I have no idea."

"You know, when I met you, I thought you were an idiot. Now I think you're a bigger idiot." I smacked him on the shoulder.

He winced and rubbed the tender spot. "That a good thing?"

"Yeah." I knuckled him on the other shoulder. "A very good thing."

I pushed by Basil, a smile plastered on my face, and headed for the first stop on my list. Thirty teachers. Sixty major acts of contrition. I had been a middle school beast, but oh, the lightness of coming clean.

Basil followed like a poodle, and when at last I emerged from Mrs. Watson's general music, it was finished. I ripped up my sheet and stuffed it in my pocket.

"Basil, you will never have the courage to do what I just did. You'll always be smooth, and you'll always be an ass." I stepped nearer. "Here's a suggestion. Open up to Crow, or stay away from her."

"What about you? Do I need to stay away from you?"

"What is it about guys? So flavor-of-the-month." I stepped back. "Forget you ever knew me."

I turned and left the school. I needed to be home early tonight. The day had come.

———

"We have trouble." Crow rocked on her bed. "Mom left for the night."

"With Jude?"

Crow shook her head. "After you went to school, Mom flipped. She said she needed time to think. She'll be back tomorrow morning."

That's not how it went down the first time. Mom was here on Mayday. Of all the nights, on this night, she needs to be here.

"I have a bad feeling." Crow stared out her window. A late-afternoon thunderstorm boomed the sky, and the air hung heavy. Either Shane had asthma, or panic—thick and palpable—souped up my lungs.

Adele drew quietly in her sketchbook. "Crow, I think this is turning out pretty good. I'll need a story for this one."

Crow peeked at me. "I'm coming, Addy." She hopped down and sat cross-legged by her sister. Addy rested her head on Crow's shoulder, and I cried . . . tears that made no sense. I came back to help Addy, but as I watched the sisters, my heart broke for Crow. She gave up her life—her carefree childhood, her passion to write, her rightful place in this family—all she sacrificed for duty and love. She was more than a hero. I mean, I was. Once again, it was so clear.

I turned, as sappy emotion wouldn't sit well with Crow. Behind me, Crow began.

"That's an impressive boat. Okay, once upon a time there was a ship, sailing on the Endless Sea."

"Who's on it?" Addy jumped in. "I need the characters."

"You'll find out. The crew was a bunch of scoundrels. Pirate types. Years ago, in the darkness of night, they attacked the boat, set its rightful captain onto a deserted island, and sailed out into deep waters.

"It was a harsh crew, except for one maiden, beautiful and kind. Truth told, she wasn't a pirate at all, but the child of the captain."

Addy interrupted. "Make a happy ending, just this once."

"Happy ending. So young was the maiden that she could not remember her father's fate, and soon her gentleness won over the crew. Even the cruelest man treated her kindly. But of those on board, her closest friend was not one of the pirates, but a troll.

He lived belowdecks with the rats. Only the maiden visited him. Only the maiden spoke to him. Only the maiden loved him."

Crow paused, and Addy spoke. "Did he love her back?"

"Oh, yes. He loved her back."

Thunder rumbled in the distance, and Crow looked up. "A storm, furious and violent, swept down from the East, catching the ship unawares. The boat experienced a lashing: the mast broke in two; the hull split; and the men scrambled for lifeboats.

"But not the maiden. She climbed into the hold, where the troll sat, half covered with water. 'Come! Quickly! I won't leave this ship without you.'

"Coaxed on, the troll rose, and together they climbed onto the deck. But the ship listed, and the two tumbled. They were alone. The lifeboats and crew were gone, and all they had was each other."

"You said this was going to end up all right," Addy said.

Crow nodded. "I did promise that. As they huddled together now near death as they had in life, a lightning bolt struck the ship, the hull broke into pieces. They dropped toward the sea, and bounced."

"Bounced?"

"Bounced. Like we did on the trampoline. Bounced. But not high. They'd fallen into a raft."

"It's the dad, the captain, right?" Addy squeezed Crow's arm. "The dad came back for them."

"No, not the father."

"Then who was it? Who saved them?"

Crow glanced up at me and smiled gently. "I'm not sure. That, perhaps, you'll find out in part two."

"I'm never . . ." Addy swatted Crow with the sketchbook. "I hate it when you do that."

Crow rejoined me on the bed.

"A raft?" I asked.

"It fit the story."

I took Crow's hand as another crack of thunder shook the house. "We need to sleep in the tree house tonight."

"Addy still gets freaked by storms. She'll never go." Crow's jaw tightened. "No, the three of us will be okay in here. I've brought food. Nobody leaves the room until morning." She raised her eyebrows. "Help me set it up."

We shoved Crow's bed in front of the door, lugged the dresser behind it.

"What are you doing?" Addy asked.

"Uh. Special rearranging for the night." Crow forced a smile. "We're all going to sleep in your bed."

Addy eyed her mattress, and then quieted. "It'll be cramped." She peered toward the window. "But I'm not too excited about this storm."

"This is why we're going to stay close." Crow glanced at me, and I tried my best to look confident. "It'll pass. They always do."

Eight o'clock turned to nine and then ten. Outside, the storm intensified. Rain clanked off the gutters, and peals of thunder rattled the window.

We huddled on Addy's bed. She had long ago fallen asleep between us. Crow looked down at her, then over at me. She reached out her hand. "I'm glad you're here."

"Me—"

The doorknob clicked and turned.

"This is no good," I whispered. "There's nobody to hear us."

"Open the door, girls." Jude's rough voice pushed in. "The storm is bad. You're welcome to sleep in my room if you're afraid."

Crow looked at me. "No!" she said. "Go away."

"What have you placed in front of this door?" The bed and dresser shook as the door opened and closed an inch.

"He's pushing," I hissed. "He's going to get in soon enough."

Crow's wide eyes scanned the room. "My knife."

"No, that doesn't stop him. Trust me. We need to get out." I jumped off the bed, raised the blinds. Rain pounded on the outside sill. "We all race to the tree house. He can't follow us up there. He doesn't fit."

Crow hopped off the bed and threw open the window. Rain splattered into the room, and more thunder shook the house. She scrambled beside Adele, shook her shoulders gently. "Sis, I need you to wake up." Slowly, Addy sat and rubbed her eyes.

The dresser rocked and jiggled, inching farther into the room. Jude's fingers reached in. "Open this door!"

"What's happening?" Addy stared at the shaking furniture.

I pushed back against the dresser, but my weight was no match for Jude's strength. "Follow me." I bounded across the room and climbed out the window into the pouring rain. I turned and stuck my head back inside and reached out my hands.

"Addy." Crow lugged her off the bed. "Do you see Shane? I need you to go to her. She's going to take you to the tree house. It's not safe here. We need to get to the tree house as fast as we can."

She shook her head and grabbed Crow around the neck. Thunder boomed. "I'm not going out there now."

"You are." Crow hauled her toward the window. "Trust me. You need to trust me that it will be all right. Shane in front of you; me behind you."

"Give me your hand!" I screamed, and reached for Adele's arm. "That's good. I'll be with you the whole way."

Behind them, Jude's head poked through the door. "Do not go out that window!"

Crow turned, saw him, and lifted Adele. I pulled and Crow pushed, and we squeezed Addy through the opening. She landed with a wet thud and ducked beneath the eaves. "I want to go inside! This is insane!"

Crow squeezed out the window, grabbed Adele around the shoulder, and the three of us scrambled across the lawn beneath the strobe-light sky.

"I hate this! What are we doing this for?" Adele wriggled and hit and pulled free as Crow slipped to her knees. Addy raced back toward the open window of the house.

"No, Adele!" I chased after her, watched in horror as she stuck her head back into the room. Strong hands grabbed her shoulders and pulled her inside. Jude's satisfied face slammed the window and pulled the shade.

Crow beat on the glass.

"Addy. I'm coming, Addy!"

I scanned the backyard, came up empty, and ran to the side of the house. I scooped up a paving stone, stumbled back, and yanked Crow aside. I flung the stone, and shards exploded into the night.

"Stop! No, that hurts!" Addy screamed from inside.

"He's got the bookshelf in front of the window!" Crow's eyes were frantic. "Bathroom!" I ran for another paving stone, sloshed back, and handed it to Crow.

She ripped off the screen and smashed the glass. She struck that window, again and again, until a large hole, jagged and dripping, appeared. Crow leaped up and disappeared. I struggled after her, tumbled to the bathroom floor, and raced into the hall.

And paused.

The sound was so foreign to the home, I hardly recognized it. A weeping, heavy and terrible. Jude's sobs filled his room, forced their way through the closed door and into the hall, rising above the din of the storm.

The Monster wept.

I broke free and charged toward our bedroom. I squeezed into the room and froze.

The bookshelf by the window had been pulled away, and Crow's torso stretched outside. In the distance, faint and thin, Addy was calling.

"Crow? Where are you, Crow?" Over and over in the

storm. I heard her name, my name. Crow jumped back out, and I walked, stiff and gasping, to the sill. A numbness I knew so well returned, and I leaned out into the rain, let myself fall forward onto the ground. Droplets, once warm and firm on my skin, turned cold.

"It can't have happened. It can't—" I looked up, while the entire night wept. In the middle of the yard, Addy stumbled toward Crow, her pajamas ripped, her legs wobbly. Crow caught Addy in her arms, and the thunder stole Addy's words.

But not the look on her face. Each flash of lightning showed the pain.

My sister in pain.

"What did he do to you?" Crow screamed.

Addy shook her head and squeezed Crow tighter.

"Get her into the tree house!" I called, staggering to my feet.

Crow stared at me.

"Go! Go!"

She led Addy to the ladder. Addy climbed up, and Crow glanced at me again . . . and collapsed, splashing face-first into a puddle. She did not move. I ran toward her, lifted her face out of the mud, and stroked her hair.

"Oh, Crow—"

"She slipped through my fingers. I had her safe in my hands. . . ." Her face darkened. "I need my knife."

"No." My head fell onto her chest. "Not tonight. Tonight, Addy needs us."

Crow's eyes opened wide, and she stumbled to her feet and climbed the ladder.

I followed without words or purpose. There was nothing I could do, nothing I could say.

How could I have failed again?

I crawled out of the rain and into a lonely place and grabbed the top blanket off the folded pile.

I sat where I first had met Crow. My vision blurred, and I blinked and looked around the tree house. Mittens from Sadie balled up in a corner, while the two sisters huddled together.

"Please, Addy," Crow choked through tears. "What did he do to you?"

"I don't know." Addy sobbed. "I don't know. He held me on his lap. His hands, they were everywhere. On top . . ." Her shaking hand raised to her mouth, and she whispered, "Underneath." She peeked down at her ripped pajamas. "Then glass broke, and he screamed and dropped me and ran out. I wish Mom was here."

My head fell back with a thud. Had it not been for my theatrics this morning, Mom would have been.

Mayday came after all.

"Addy, I should have told you so much more." Crow

stroked her sister's hair. "I should have been clear. I knew what he wanted, and I thought I could keep it away and didn't want you to live worried. But maybe if *you* would've told Mom, she would have listened."

Addy nestled in tighter. "You knew he would try this? The knife, it wasn't for all those sandwiches you brought into the room?"

Crow squeezed tight her eyes.

"And the bed, you weren't really afraid of sleepwalking. That's not why you moved it." Addy whispered, "And I bet you're not afraid of the dark."

Addy looked up, grabbed a blanket, and drew it close. She breathed deeply. "Crow, I love you."

Fresh tears traced down Crow's cheeks, and we sat, hurting and healing, beneath the storm.

"Finish the story," Addy said. "The boat one. The maiden and the troll were in a raft. They're safe."

Crow glanced around the tree house, her gaze skipping over me. "Now? I don't think I can—"

"Please."

I scooted around the tree house next to Adele. My locket felt extraordinarily heavy, like a boulder in my pocket. I lifted it out and flipped it open.

Yellow. All hint of green was gone. Half done. Sadie said

yellow meant half done. But there was nobody left to save. I reached my arm around Adele and felt nothing.

"It was Shane." Crow sighed. "In the raft? That was supposed to be Shane."

"No," I whispered, and crawled directly in front of Addy. I tried to draw her near, tried to grasp Crow's hand with my own, but all sense of touch had faded. I was drifting into shadow.

"Addy? Crow? I'm here. I'm still here."

"Shane. Of course it was. Where did she go?" Adele dropped her gaze and pressed harder into Crow.

"She must still be in the yard. You know her. She'll be up soon. She always comes at the right time. Unlike me."

"I'm right here!" I yelled, and buried my face in my hands. When next I moved them, Sadie's face leaned over mine.

"I know, child. I know."

Sadie straightened and reached for her knitting. The back of the ambulance was as I left it—rain pounding down on the roof, Shane lying beside me. I propped myself up on an elbow. I was dry, and I was Crow.

Sadie stared over at Shane, her body wet, her arm sliced from shards of window glass and caked in blood. Sadie reached over and touched Shane's face, frozen in a look of panic.

"You sure done put your loaner through it. Appreciate you bringing her back, though."

"It wasn't my choice. You pulled me!" My voice cracked. "One thing. All I had to do was one thing. And I did nothing. I failed Addy again."

"You still missing the point. I told you before, you wasn't making the trip for her. It's a dicey proposition to alter events for others. You was introducin' too many variables. I had no choice but to bring you back. I told you, best stick to your own affairs." She looked up from her scarf. "Though in that respect you done good."

I swung to a sitting position, and the world spun.

"Take it on easy now. The process doesn't come without a bit of dizziness."

"What did I do for Crow? For me?"

"I saw a hardened girl start believing in someone again. She started believing in you, which means Crow started to believe in herself. I saw a girl full of guilt from her daddy leavin', her whole life so sure she played the main role. I don't see that anymore. She's starting to feel the truth. That's plantin' seeds. That's progress." She bustled into the front. "Come up here."

I climbed after Sadie, and together we stared at the display. Nothing had changed with Lifeless. Jude and the doctor stood at the bedside, lost in serious discussion. Adele was there, too.

"Watch." Sadie whispered.

Dr. Ambrose handed Jude a clipboard, and Jude took a pen from his pocket. Adele screamed and flew toward them. She slapped Jude across the face, then slapped the doctor. While both men bent over, palms to cheeks, she snatched the paper and ran from the room.

"Okay, that's not . . . Adele would never do that."

"That's the thing, child. You entered, set a chain of events in motion, and disappeared. Your main effect was on you, but I wouldn't bet that you was as hopeless as you thought, even with Addy." Sadie reached out her hand. "I need you to return the locket, Coraline. Wherever you end up, it can't go with you."

I stared down at it, flipped it open to be sure. "Yellow. Wait, you said that was halfway. In the dream, plenty happens after it turns yellow. I have more time." I stared at her. "Send me back again." I grabbed Sadie's knitting, stuck the locket in her face. "Are you listening? It's still yellow! I have time! You said that until the color fades to black, I can change."

"Walkabouts is intended to be second chances, not thirds or fourths." Sadie whispered. "They're gifts, really. Besides, why should I give loaners to folk who will not follow direction, who focus on everyone else's life but their own?"

"Okay, I get that, and this *is* about my life!" I lowered my voice. "Listen, please, that wasn't the only Mayday disaster.

I couldn't stop the first one. I can still stop the second."

Sadie gently reached for her needles. I snatched them out of her grasp.

She sighed. "I know what happened, saw your accident with my own eyes. But we don't use walkabouts to cheat death. We use them to make better on life."

"I can do both. Send me back and I'll give you back your knitting stuff. A trade."

My, how out of my league I now see I was. The arrogance. The folly of playing cat and mouse with Sadie's knitting may be my single dumbest act. But she was merciful.

"Supposin' I was to send you back again, when would you—"

"Winter, senior year."

"Your last year. We're clear that this is the year of *your* crash." Sadie clicked her tongue and gave a knowing nod. "If'n I send you back, I'd have some explainin' to do." She exhaled loud and long. "But you are right. The locket's at yellow. You have some time." She paused. "But not much. Be still."

This command made no sense until I tried to move. Muscles no longer obeyed. Inside my chest, there was a vacuum. No heartbeat. No breathing. I sat there every bit the mannequin. Sadie reached over and plucked her knitting from limp hands, and I was released.

She raised her yarn in front of my face, and her eyes flashed. "Some liberties best not to take. Get in back."

My eyes widened, and I leaped through the door.

And winced.

"Now, there's a guy back here. I'd say he's eighteen or nineteen. He's good looking but, wait, no. You're not sending me back as a guy? That's uh, not going to work."

"It'll work just fine. While you was frozen up front, I done searched for a young lady, but we's fresh out of suitables right now. But don't you fret. Like I said last time, we've altered the body."

"Can't you alter him to a female?"

Sadie turned somber. "We can only go so far. Here's a scarf for the trip. It'll be even colder."

I eased down onto the cot. "Does he have a name?"

"He did. But I suggest you keep using Shane, for ease. Remember, when red turns black, you're coming back, this time for good. No argument."

"Just give me until Mayday. I can make things right." I peeked over at Shane. "I think."

For a second time, I joined hands with a corpse.

"Good-bye, Coraline."

CHAPTER 11

THE THOUGHTS OF C. RAINE

See things from the boy's point of view.
Sir Alec Baldwin

COLD. I FIRST FELT IT ON MY ANKLES AND WRISTS—a surrounding, aching cold—and I, Shane, opened my eyes.

All was white, and my mind traveled to Mexico.

During my junior year, three disciples and I traveled there for spring break. The others were in it for the guys. They flew thousands of miles to tan their bodies by day, and slowly lose their minds—and then much more—by night.

I kept my skin covered and shielded by black.

After all, I went for the ocean.

The raw power of waves splashing forever toward me, crashing on the rocks, pooling, spraying, caressing. Then leaving—no commitment sought, no damage done, no defilement left.

Chekov said, "The sea has neither meaning nor pity." I don't know. I could do an ocean.

A twisted idea? Sure. But Minnesota inclines the soul toward the coasts.

Now snow—that was common as spit. I was born beneath it, raised surrounded by it, expected to shovel it and trudge through it, only to watch it turn dirt black along the roads. White disappeared. Dirtied, defiled, contaminated. Every flake abandoned me when air turned warm. Snow, the ultimate tease.

But today, that did not matter. I spread wide my arms and opened myself up, let the cool flakes fall on my warm tongue. This seesaw of sensation made every chill glorious.

I glanced down to where I stood, my feet atingle in twelve inches of powdery white.

But my neck was warm, toasted by a scarf.

"Thanks, Sadie . . . Oh, no."

This was not a passing morning voice. My words rumbled husky and low. I cleared my throat and looked myself over. "Seriously?"

I peeked down at my jeans, unzipped my fly, winced, and took a peek.

"Whoa. That's just not right."

"Is there a problem, young man?"

I whipped around, hands still clasped on my briefs.

Officer Dewey and an unfamiliar cop frowned from inside their squad.

"You lose something?" Dewey chuckled. Totally a Basil thing to say.

"No. I, uh, I found something."

Dewey nodded. "I certainly hope so. It's the spot I would have directed you to. It sure appeared as if you were on the way to dropping your drawers. You know there are some rules against that, son?"

I rezipped my pants and tucked in my shirt. "Yeah, I'm good. Just a little cold is all."

Dewey opened his door and pushed out. I faced him eye to eye. A very cool feeling.

"No jacket." He circled me one way and then the other. "Do you have someplace to go? Maybe a name, son?" Dewey paused and held out his hand. "I'd like to see some ID."

"It's Shane, and I, uh, no to the ID part, but yeah to the someplace-to-go part." I glanced around. *Where am I?*

Here, I struck a bit of fortune. Yes, the road looked familiar, but there were no houses. Just snow-covered buildings and a small sign: HOPE HOME FOR BOYS. OPEN DECEMBER 1. The boys home had indeed opened its doors during my senior year. That's all my memory needed.

Our neighborhood had fought against Hope Home's construction. Consensus was the build would transport "troubled and violent youth" into the area. The Monster had, ironically, been one of the project's most vocal critics.

"The people of this fine community pay plenty in property taxes." Jude waited for the mumbled agreement to hush, and he peered confidently around the City Council room. "We work hard to see that our standard of living remains unblemished."

Unblemished. A nasty word—just a side note.

He continued, "We understand the plight of the boys. We feel their pain. And we feel it's in the best interest of everyone to let the boys run around elsewhere. Perhaps across town in a less-established neighborhood."

I sat in the back of the council room. I loved the drama, but the sight of Jude made me gag.

"You'd rather see a pack of boys loose in the streets than monitored in a decent home with a curfew?" I called.

Heads turned, and neighbors murmured. Afterward, Councilman Harris told me my comment shifted the direction of debate. It also would end my life as I knew it, but foresight's never twenty-twenty.

The neighborhood lost. The home was built, completed before Christmas.

I stared, wide-eyed, at a waiting Officer Dewey. Mayday was five months away.

Basil and Mel were still my friends.

Crow was a living, breathing girl.

Adele was getting cozy with Will Kroft, the most infamous resident of Hope Home.

Do I ever have someplace to go!

I poked over my shoulder. "I'm heading in to apply at the new Hope residence. What do you think?" I stroked Sadie's gift. "Was the scarf a good interview choice?"

Dewey's partner spoke up. "Gloves and a coat might've served you better."

Both officers slowly climbed back in the squad car. "Suggestion. Keep your hands off the fly. Makes a bad first impression." Dewey slapped the outside of the car and pulled away.

I watched their squad car turn out of sight, lifted strong arms to the sky, and shouted. I pumped my fists and hollered again.

Is this primal thing what all guys feel?

I checked my hands, callused and worked. "What did you do, Shane? When you were living. What did you do?"

Good-looking guy. I bet he did it well.

"Okay, here it starts." I trudged toward the Hope Home

office and jammed my hands in my pockets. My right hand found the locket, my left a crinkled five-dollar bill.

I'm not thirteen anymore, Sadie. This isn't enough for a gum ball.

———

My psychology teacher once erupted on a gender rant. "Females and males are exactly the same. Same, same, same, except for body parts." I had no information to counter the assertion—our biology dissection schedule didn't include boy and girl brains.

Yet I'd done a fair amount of thinking, and the idea struck me as wrong. Give a girl and guy the same parents. Feed them the same food. Discipline them equally and throw them into the same school. It didn't matter. The guy would end up, well, a guy. The reason for this aside you will now see.

I reached the main office and stepped inside. I stomped snow off my shoes and brushed off my jeans. Frozen feet screamed to prickly life. The office was warm and pleasant enough, with plush chairs, nice pictures, and a cute receptionist.

I blinked hard, and she smiled at me over the counter, gently biting her lip and twirling her hair. *That lip-biting thing does work.*

Her gaze fastened to me, wandered up and down, and I

peeked to make sure the fly was upped. Good there.

I straightened and swaggered up to her.

Dammit, Shane. You've got to be kidding.

She was pretty. Really pretty. I put her at twenty and wondered where she lived. If she lived there alone.

She's a girl, you stupid body!

"I'm looking for something to do." I rested an elbow on the counter and flexed a bicep. Totally posing. I wanted to throw up.

She tongued the inside of her cheek (a squirrelly maneuver with no seductive effect), reached down, and raised a stack of papers to the counter. "I have an opening. New in town?"

"Back after a long absence."

"What about a place to stay? Here could be good."

I pulled the papers close to me. "I just need work. This is the application?"

"Yeah, it is. A cottage on site comes with the job, you know."

I cleared my throat. "So I could live right here."

"Alone," she said, her lips curling. "Could be interesting, don't you think?"

"Family teacher assistant." I read the job description. "I don't think this is for me." I held up my palms. "I think I work with my hands. Repair or maintenance? Got anything like that?"

She reached over the counter and gently took hold of my hands, cradling them in her own. "Oh, I'll find something to do with these hands."

Is this double entendre making you sick? To recount it now, yeah, it has a nauseating effect, but I tell you, then I was into it.

"The house needs the position filled soon." She sat back down. "Mr. Loumans is desperate for some help. We opened early, and the kids are time intensive."

A place to stay at Hope Home for Boys, a chance to keep an eye on Will, who by now had hooks in Addy? I grabbed a pen and attacked the paperwork.

> **Name**: *Shane Owen*
>
> **Age:** I scanned myself and shrugged. *Eighteen*
>
> **Education:** *Central High School*
>
> **Home Address:**
>
> **Work Address:**
>
> **References:**

"These questions get tougher." I muttered. "I can't do this."

The girl stood and looked over my paper. "Those hands of yours will stay unemployed with an application like this. We need to make you even more, well, desirable." She crossed out eighteen and wrote twenty-one.

"Let me handle you and your app." She flipped over one

of her cards. "Just give me a number where I can reach you."

My gaze darted. "Well, that depends on when you're going to call. Could I just check back tomorrow?"

She set down her pen and cocked her head. "You're kind of a mystery."

"You have no idea."

Moments passed, and finally she raised her brows. "Okay, Shane Owen. Tomorrow it is. Wait, are you really still in school?"

"That depends on whether or not I land this job."

"Love that." She flipped over her card and slid it across the counter. "Keep my contact. In case something comes up, or if it doesn't." She reclined in her roller chair. "Call my cell."

"Right." I grabbed the card and backed toward the door. My heel caught on the doormat and I stumbled, regained my footing, and offered an awkward grin.

That girl shook her head, breathed deep, and beamed from ear to ear. "Perfect."

Tripping makes me perfect? Or my grin is perfect? What are you thinking?

I'm a guy. No wonder I'm suddenly clueless.

I pushed out and pocketed her information. Wind howled around me. The number on the card could well provide me a place for the night. But that seemed way wrong, at least to the Crow part of me.

Where to sleep . . .

"The Shack."

I trudged toward the bus stop, replaying my stumble, wondering why two minutes with a no-name receptionist now captured my thoughts. But somewhere during the walk, my mind hopped off that track and I dug for my Abe Lincoln.

A fifty would have been much more thoughtful.

Here my mind cleared, focused. Sadie's warnings aside, there were things to undo by Mayday. A twisted chain of events must be broken. Unlike my first walkabout, the list of those involved was long. Yet, alter the course of a few lives, and links in that chain shattered.

Any links would do.

Busted links mean a prevented accident.

My mind replayed the causes of my demise, and the steps to my survival.

Given: Will had bragged about what he wanted to do to Addy on May 1, prom night.

Given: Only trusting Addy believed it was a rumor, forcing me to take action.

But.

1. If Adele doesn't date Will from Hope Home, Crow doesn't need to protect her from him.

2. If Crow doesn't need to protect her, she won't need to speed Will away from Addy on the night of the prom.

3. If she doesn't need to speed him away, she won't clip the train.

4. And Lifeless will never appear, and Crow won't vegetate, and she will have zero urge to flirt with female receptionists.

I peeked over my shoulder toward Hope Home, to where Monster Number 2 lived. Working with Will and keeping him far from Addy would truly be . . .

Perfect.

"I really need that job."

The bus pulled up, and I stepped inside.

This would be a lot easier if I had some help. My plan was complicated; the number of people whose lives I needed to disrupt? Considerable. A stranger in my own past, I needed somebody I could trust, somebody with connections. A confidant, a smooth operator to lend a hand.

Only one person had access to all the players in this drama.

I knew just where to find him.

CHAPTER 12

THE THOUGHTS OF C. RAINE

The belly rules the mind.
Spanish proverb

I STEPPED OFF THE BUS AT THE CORNER OF HENNEPIN AND RACINE across from Crow and Basil's workplace. A pea-green snowmobile fishtailed to a curbside stop. I glanced from the machine to the corner where, standing not twenty feet before me, was Basil.

"My help," I whispered.

He paid no attention to either my bus or the snowmobile, his lips moving to the words of the book he read. I'll come back to Basil, but first a word about winter driving.

Glare ice coated Hennepin Avenue, and cars slid by us sideways and backward.

I stepped back from the curb. Minneapolis drivers were typically a sensible lot in winter, so different than out-of-state fools who filled ditches with their spinouts. But all local sensibilities went out the window at Hennepin and Racine. A bewildering mix of mountain bikes, skiers, snowmobiles, and four-wheel drives shared the road with more common fare, making it the most dangerous corner one could stand near.

Which is why Basil loved it.

Why he didn't mind wearing a sheet of cardboard on his front, and another on his back.

Why he graciously accepted his role as the Shack's Hennepin and Racine Human Pizza Sign.

The rider of the snowmobile hopped off and hollered in a muffled mix of English, Spanish, and Curse. "Blast you, pizza sign!"

Basil briefly peeked up from his book, cocked his head, and the screamer paused.

Basil sighed. He often did that. The past five years had been good to him. He turned out too smart and too good looking and too, well, just too, to end up a sandwich sign. He knew it. But when cursed with Basil's luck, you grasp any job that comes your way, even if it's a whisker above unemployment.

The sled's engine fell silent, and the rider rounded the front with a full head of steam. Whatever the origin of his anger, there would be no escape for Basil. His piece of frozen ground was the size of a bathroom mat, with a railing behind and a rush-hour skating rink in front. It was a ten-minute ordeal to gently remove the sandwich sign, dodge the cars, and reach the Shack, home of jelly-bean pizza.

The guy was still screaming. I slowed my steps and strained my ears.

"Woman defiler! You're a predatory pizza sign!"

Sounds like Basil's been busy again.

Basil's bad luck ended when it came to girls. It always had. I, above all people, knew this, though peering from inside Shane's male body, I couldn't understand any of Basil's magnetic hold.

I stared at the Shack across the road and let memories flood.

Basil once had a respectable job. With me. Inside. We flirted and washed dishes and flirted—more, I believed, to pass time than to express anything real.

Until one day, Mr. Hovanitz reached around Basil's shoulder.

"My fellow American, I need an outside sales rep. You will be my Great Communicator."

He said it was a promotion. He said it involved travel, and this was true, but only on a technicality. The position did sound important. Basil volunteered.

The next week, business at the Shack plummeted. Mr. H. blamed Basil for embodying "disinterested signage."

He had that right.

I trudged forward through the snow, closer to the scene. Beyond the snowmobile rider—the cursing one—beyond the slipping, swerving vehicles, the Whole Foods parking lot filled with shouts and flashing lights, and both Basil and the rider paused to look. I'd never seen so many angry vegans.

Suddenly, I had no idea why I was here. What did I expect Basil to do for me? I backtracked and stood against the outside of the glass bus stop enclosure and watched my best friend.

He didn't look back.

Maybe I'm invisible again.

I waved at a driver. She blew me a kiss and slid on by.

I sighed. "Still good."

"I'm talking to you, weasel. Basil, you're a snake in the grass!" The snowmobile rider kicked the machine.

Very hard. Over and over.

Basil winced and lowered his book. "Okay, that's enough. Foot off my sled!"

He adjusted his triangular pizza hat, took another look at Whole Foods, and returned to *The Spy Master*. I suggested he try Nietzsche, but Basil loved mysteries. He said they helped him escape the existential insanity of our real lives.

He'd love the mess I was in.

"I should kill you! I should do it right now!" The snowmobiler steamed.

"Um, hm." The Spy Master was deep undercover. I wanted snowmobile guy to shut up. I needed Basil to see me. To see the *me* in me. I needed to be recognized by somebody.

The rider wouldn't go.

He couldn't. Couldn't stop grunting. Grunting and pulling. Pulling and bending. He was bent in two, clawing at his helmet, still stuck on his ears.

It looked three sizes too small.

Then I remembered: Sergio.

The memory yanked from me a laugh, deep and manly. Basil and I had been with Sergio when he purchased that helmet from the PowerLodge.

"It looks small and girly," Basil said. "Besides, why not wait until you get a snowmobile?"

Sergio turned the helmet over in his hands. "That'll come soon. What do you think, Crow?"

I shrugged. "It does have that peach, retro vibe, if that's what you're going for."

Sergio stepped nearer to me and raised his eyebrows. "Do you like peach?"

"I like peaches." I broke into laughter.

"I'll take it!" Sergio marched to the counter and plunked down a fistful of dollars.

His head has been paying for that purchase ever since.

Sergio fought those ears—the ones the size of pancakes—and the helmet released with a suctioned pop. He gasped and massaged those pancakes and reached for the basket bungeed behind the seat.

Basil dropped his book. "Calm down, Sergio. Get off the road. You're going to get killed." He reached out his hand. "Give me the keys. There's stupid and there's this."

Horns blared as cars swerved around the sled. Sergio didn't care.

He was driven. Or obsessed. There's not much of a difference.

Sergio removed something long and green and reared back. Basil penguin-stepped sideways.

"I had to pay for the last sign myself. I can't afford—"

A vegetable *thunked* against his thigh.

Basil scowled and rubbed his leg. "That felt like a zucchini!" He lifted his head just in time to take an eggplant on the cheek.

"Home wrecker!" Sergio reached for another vegetable.

"I didn't touch her!"

"You probably did more than that."

An acorn squash to Basil's temple.

"Is this about Crow again? We work together," Basil shouted. "We closed together. She was in her mood and asked me to walk her home."

"At two A.M.? Things happen at two A.M. How come she doesn't speak to me anymore?"

What would I say to you?

"C never speaks to you, and you're an idiot."

"Now she's 'C.' Already have a pet name for her, huh?"

Beans showered. One lodged in Basil's ear.

"That does it." Basil whipped his ear bean toward the street, ducked out of his sign, hoisted it above his head, and charged.

"Basil?"

I turned slowly and stared across the street.

It was me.

Crow's voice cut through traffic and grabbed the three of us by the neck. For an instant, everybody froze. She stood in front of the Shack and wiped her hands on her apron. "Are you okay?"

It's me. I'm alive.

"See," Sergio double-fisted some carrots and shook them toward Basil. "She cares for you!" A volley of vegetables rained down on Basil. Carrot, carrot, green pepper. "She wants to know how you are." Red pepper.

Basil swatted away airborne produce. "Fine, C, I'm fine. Sergio's just returning my snowmobile."

Basil took several cauliflower heads to the chest and groin. The last dropped him into fresh powder.

Two squad cars pulled up, parked in front and behind

the snowmobile. Three officers and an angry guy in a Whole Foods apron joined Basil on the corner.

"That's him," squeaked Apron Man. "He ran off with a basket of organic vegetables—"

"The pizza-sign kid?"

"No, him!" Apron Man pointed at Sergio, who took off on foot.

I knew they wouldn't catch him.

They knew it, too. The cops were weighty and Sergio was quick, and soon he blended in with thousands of skiers on Lake Calhoun Parkway.

Apron Man started a pathetic sniffle. "But what about my eggplant?" He sure loved his vegetables. I remembered thinking that from when I watched this scene from Crow's position across the street.

He bent over and gently lifted the purplish skin. "This eggplant has been terrorized."

How do you terrorize a vegetable?

The police shrugged and tagged the snowmobile.

"That's my sled!" Basil screamed. "My dad's a cop, and he's comin' after you."

"Sure, kid." A policeman bent over and plucked an apple out of the snow. He examined it, rubbed it on his uniform, and took a chomp. "If your dad was a cop, he'd have told you about leaving sleds parked in snow-emergency routes.

Have a good day." He hopped into the squad car and fishtailed away.

Basil kicked his splattered sign and gazed toward the parkway.

Basil was my best friend.

His sign was a mess.

This had been my life.

"What are you staring at?"

I shook free from my daydream, blinked, and shuffled my feet. I hadn't moved in minutes.

"Uh, the show."

"Show's over." Basil grabbed the ticket, ripped it in half, and inspected his snowmobile—his pride and joy.

He doesn't know me. How do I change the future of complete strangers?

I breathed deeply and wandered across the street toward the smell of pizza. I slipped inside the Shack, grabbed a handful of free peppermints, and veered right into the bathroom.

Crow was supposed to clean the unisex every other hour, but I—I mean, she—rarely did.

I locked the door and collapsed in the corner, like I did in the hospital. Like I did in my bedroom at home. Somehow, corners felt right.

Why had I come? Why had I thought Basil could help?

I'd been wrong. He didn't know all the players involved in my drama.

He didn't know me.

I buried my head in my hands.

Soon I'd find sleep, but right then, I felt Lifeless.

CHAPTER 13

THE THOUGHTS OF C. RAINE

Millions of spiritual creatures walk the earth.
Unseen, both when we wake and when we sleep.
John Milton, *Paradise Lost*

I WOKE TO A NAMELESS HOUR, AND A SILENCE, THICK AND WEIGHTY.

This was disconcerting. My early years spent stethoscoping each nighttime moment, listening for anomalies that screamed, "Boots on, Monster comes," had turned my nights into drawn-back arrows. Though Addy no longer needed me at night—Jude's visits came to a screeching halt after the first Mayday's horror—the slightest of sounds still caused me to fire, to wake.

Still, sound grounded me, provided mile markers through the dark.

The eerie quiet of the bathroom held no passing of time, and I was terrified. I'd not felt time's flow beside Lifeless either. It was, perhaps, a wandering soul's greatest curse—stuck on earth in a perpetual now.

But both the previous shell and the present Shane could change this. Within them, as before, time passed, events flowed. Life happened.

At least outside this bathroom.

I stood and stretched.

Stiff.

It described my neck and my back and the drainpipe I'd used as a pillow. I washed my face and gazed into the mirror, thankful for this stranger steeled for the tasks ahead.

Keep Will Kroft from my sister. Keep the relationship from starting. No start? No reason to end it, or end me.

I rubbed my face, felt stubble on my chin, and exhaled hard. How many shells like me were out there? How many souls were on their walkabouts? How many people I've known weren't really—

"Do not neglect to show hospitality to strangers, for thereby some have entertained angels unawares." The quote muscled in, and I damped down my hair. Well, I'm no angel. Maybe it applies to souls, too.

⁓

I was sixteen when Francine decided to marry. It wasn't a future I had seen for my second cousin—she wasn't exactly marriage material, whatever that is. But she snagged some poor soul, and before he could flee, the date was set: October 31.

You knew it wasn't going to be a lasting union.

Francine lived in St. Cloud, an hour's drive away, and due to popularity issues, she had tapped Addy and me for bridesmaids. I saw the mustard-yellow, leaf-print "happy-dress" I was to wear, and my stomach turned. Adele joined me in Mom's bathroom minutes later. She bested me and actually threw up, though her sickness had more to do with the Monster's comment: "You'll look good in that, Adele."

The wedding rehearsal fell on October 30. So did snow, a thick, heavy road-closing surprise that canceled Halloween and drove us to curse the state we lived in. Unfortunately, it wasn't enough to cancel the wedding.

Adele stayed in St. Cloud overnight as the snowfall deepened. Wee hours filled with second thoughts and nervous giggles weren't my thing, and I hopped on I-94 to risk the ride home. The highway was closed. There were no other vehicles, though this could be inaccurate; I couldn't see out the front windshield. I opened my driver's-side window, stuck out my head, and drove straight. It worked for sixty miles.

My exit approached; I sensed it. I could not see the sign. I could not see anything. I waited, waited. The snow eased; surely I was crossing beneath the underpass. I feathered the brake, fishtailed forward, and eased right.

Too sharp. I missed the off-ramp and plummeted down

into the bowl of snow. In nautical terms, my car plunged thirty feet below sea level, or ramp level. In any case, I was way down there, the snow covering my hood. I pounded the wheel and cursed, knowing I'd be buried alive and found dead in mustard yellow.

I removed the key from the ignition and lowered my head.

A hand smacked my window, and I jumped.

I watched the glove brush away snow, and wave. I saw the face, kind of. It was a guy, I knew that, but in the blizzard more details were impossible. Twenty seconds later, I felt a *clunk*, and my car jerked forward. Up, up. I plowed forward and up until I came to a gentle stop. Caked-on snow fell from my windows, and I pushed out my door.

There was nobody—no tow truck, no wandering do-gooder—nobody. My car rested safely on the street. I turned and looked down into the bowl of snow, at the ten-foot drift I'd been in. There were no tracks, no sign I'd been there. Only the foot of snow piled on my hood provided proof of my sanity.

Believe what you will, but understand why I might be more open than most to the possibility of wandering souls, passing angels, things I can't see. One hauled me from a ditch, then disappeared. Maybe his locket turned black and his walkabout was over. Maybe Sadie yanked him.

That's more than a little weird.

That's *Twilight Zone* material.

I leaned toward the mirror. "Crow. Are you in there?"

Many of my emotions were still mine, were still Crow's. Adele, I loved her. Jude, disgusting as ever.

But my thoughts, they were foreign. A hard drive that would have been completely unexplainable by my exchangeable-body-parts psych teacher.

1. I will wear the same clothes today. Apparently, that was okay.

2. Today, I will take no shower. That seemed reasonable as well.

3. That girl from Hope Home. She wasn't listed on the job's benefit package, but she should have been.

I splashed more water on my face. I'd become a hound.

Three clicks, followed by grinding and a low hum. The heat kicked on. The furnace whirred to life at six A.M., the same time Frankie stumbled in to open up.

Get out of here.

I unlatched the door and peeked out into the still of the Shack, slipping quickly into the empty dining area. Shadowy images of Mr. Hovanitz stared at me from every wall.

I paused and smirked. He'd hired me as a waitress, which had lasted one day. Apparently, he didn't like how my basic black clashed with the Shack's standard brown uniform. I was demoted: first to cashier, then to pizza maker, and finally to dishwasher. That was fine by me, as I'd never pass on a chance to clean up.

I did my job well. I dreamed of no reason to leave. Adele had college aspirations, maybe a doctor or a vet. By eighteen, my passion for writing had devolved into dark poetry, filled with anarchist tendencies and philosophical traps. Not much market for that.

But Addy, she was emerging beautifully, and my protective services were no longer needed. I'd lived to be her bodyguard. Now my empty heart idolized her from afar, waiting until she would call on me again. And then I'd be here, ready.

Cleaning dishes.

No time to reminisce. My prize lay behind the counter: a garbage bag bulging with breadsticks. Soon, the food-shelf truck would pick up yesterday's leftovers. A gift for the hungry. I figured myself more than deserving.

I tore at the bag and removed hunks of hardened bread. I scurried to the fridge, stuffing bread into my cheeks and swallowing whole.

It turned out that Shane was a pig who double-fisted his food. I bent over and removed two packs of dunking sauce. If I'd had time, I would've whipped up a jelly-bean pizza, but Frankie was rarely late.

Finally, from the back room, I grabbed Basil's Shack

jacket, the one he wore on the corner. I would not wear the pizza hat.

Warm and fed, I pushed out the back door, tramping around to the street.

In the darkness of early morning, Hennepin Avenue bustled, and I paused at the curb. I knew every coffee shop and boarded-up business, but they felt foreign. Life inside this Shane had me mystified.

Maybe I wasn't Crow. Maybe I never had been. Maybe I had always been Shane and I just woke from a bizarre sleep in which I dreamed up another life.

Or maybe I'd watched *The Matrix* one time too many.

I urged my feet forward, and they shuffled onto icy tar. The glass frame of the bus stop glistened beneath a streetlamp's glow. Shadowy figures shifted inside, and I weaved between cars and approached.

Two guys, loud and hooded, waited on the bench.

One black. One white.

They cursed and jostled, and my stomach flipped because even I knew my limits. There were places girls didn't venture before daylight and places they did. This was a didn't.

I slowed my steps, glanced over my male frame, and relaxed.

I sat down and grunted.

The guys grew still, small, and grunted back. They slumped on the bench and slipped into their poser faces.

We grunted some more, which was amazing, if only because I understood everything. Note to self. Guys are bilingual, conversant in at least two languages: English and Grunt.

If these guys only knew.

—

I stepped into the Hope Home office, glanced at the receptionist, and felt my gaze drop eight inches.

Stop that.

"I'm here."

Reese looked up. That turned out to be her name. Her nameplate was the first thing I noted, given its . . . prominent placement. That and she was dressed really good.

"You're early, and that's okay . . . usually." She bit her lip again and walked around the desk. *Okay, that's way too much leg for December.* Reese was trying really hard. Way too hard. Inside, a switch flipped from attack mode to escape. Crazy.

But I couldn't run away from Will Kroft. Sadie had set me down in the perfect place, next to the kid who wanted to destroy my sister. I'd do a better job of neutralizing this time around. Unlike my first trip back, I had months to intervene.

I pried my gaze off Reese's legs. "I'll wait."

Reese raised her hand to her face and started chewing a nail, a move that tilts toward compulsive and away from sexy. "That's not the best idea. Mr. Loumans—the house parent I told you about—he's dealing with a crisis right now."

I heard a shout. I knew the shout. I'd been yanking on his IV for weeks.

"What's going on?" I asked.

"It's not for me to say, or for you to know—there are privacy issues involved. I really need to ask you to leave."

A side door burst open, and in strode a determined man, followed at a distance by a cursing Will Kroft.

"Reese. We've had a breach of trust. Will denies any part in the matter, and I want to believe him, but—"

"What the hell is the breach? I never touched your damn phone." Will waved off Mr. Loumans, turned, and stomped back toward the door. "You're a joke. This place is a joke. What do I want with your piece of junk?"

I closed my eyes and imagined reaching for the IV. I felt it, grasped it. *Time to yank.*

"You'd like to call her," I said quietly, and took a seat. "You're going to use this man's phone to call her, because Mom, I mean Susan, won't take calls from your cell anymore."

I didn't look up, but basked in the glow of his silent shock. "Addy's more than you deserve, but for some reason she gives you the time of day," I scoffed. "Then again, she's a sucker for hard-luck cases. She takes in stray dogs, brings in sick birds. I'm not sure into which category of animal she places you, but she does endure your calls. But all that will change. I'll make sure of it."

I cleared my throat and glanced around the room.

All stared at me, except for Will, who had not yet turned. I would have paid good money to see his face.

Mr. Loumans rested against the counter, his face deep in thought.

"So," I continued, "what's not clear about the phone incident? Do I need to go into detail? The first time you took this man's phone, Jude answered. The Monster gave you to Addy, and you talked for about two hours. About yourself." I paused. "Little side note: ask a girl a question here and there, and then shut up and listen. They like that. But back to your eternal call, Addy had to go, but you called her right back— like you always do, never taking no for an answer, right?" I steamed, clenched my teeth, and kept going. "You need a phone for that. You need his personal phone. Because every call that goes into Adele's house goes through her mom, and her mom won't answer any more solicitations from Hope Home, and fortunately, Addy is smart enough not to have given you her cell number. At least not yet."

Will slowly spun, and I looked at him square. "What does she see in you anyway?"

He glanced around, and exhaled slowly.

"Give the man his phone back," I said. "Or do you want to hear more? I've got the rest of the story."

That Basil's father was a cop held distinct advantages. That he occasionally bent the rules for us, even better.

It was during one of those rule benders when I first met Will.

I was sixteen, and Basil had asked if I'd like to run "the route" with his dad. Not one to admit I had no idea what that was, I agreed.

At seven thirty, Basil and his father pulled up in the police truck.

"It's a sad duty—a necessary duty, but a sad one," Officer Dewey said as we chugged downtown.

We spent the next three hours doing pickups. Officer Dewey threw, or helped, fifteen homeless into the back of the truck, and took them to Mary Kay's shelter.

Number sixteen didn't go so smoothly.

Number sixteen was Will.

Dewey pulled beneath the Washington Bridge, and there he was, leaning back against the concrete and surrounded by shattered glass.

He wasn't alone.

A lump buried beneath a blanket rested on his lap. Another someone.

Squinting in the light, he waved Dewey off as he approached. I had to hear and cracked the window.

"You can't sleep out here, son. I have two beds left, and one has your name on it."

"No, sir. I won't come with you. But take him." He nodded down at the shape. "His feet are really bad off."

Will and Dewey helped the old man into the truck. "Listen," Will said, "I'll move on. I'll find someplace. But you got two more down by the river—one a girl about my age, and I don't think she's going to make it. You'll need an ambulance."

Dewey ran to the riverbank, and I watched Will disappear into the night. It was the last I figured I'd see of him.

When he resurfaced years later, I decided, there was no way some homeless drifter was going to set his paws on my sister. Heck, he might have killed that girl by the river.

But Will had been homeless. The fact would end up being a terrible trap for my sister. Empathy had always been Addy's one imperfection.

⌣

"Dresser," Will said. "Third drawer down. In a black sock." He exhaled slowly, his eyes narrowing.

"You can go, Will." Mr. Loumans placed his hand on Will's back. "I somewhat appreciate your honesty." He guided Will toward the door through which they'd entered minutes earlier, and then turned to me.

"And you are . . .?"

"Cr— Shane."

He looked at Reese, who smiled and commenced more lip biting. "This is the applicant I mentioned. He impressed me. My friends consider me a good judge of character. His name is Shane, and, well, you knew that."

"The Shane." Mr. Loumans stepped forward and shook my hand. Reese handed him my application. He looked it over. I did, too. It was filled out. Complete. It sure didn't look like a guy's writing.

"The spelling of your last name, O-W-E-N, is that a correct spelling, son?"

"That's right."

Mr. Loumans pitched the app in the garbage.

"Shane Owen. My new family assistant teacher."

~

I derived great pleasure from crushing Will. Having lived through his frequent phone attempts once before certainly gave me an upper hand. But my victory felt empty, like scoring a C in biology when you alone know you cheated.

Mr. Loumans didn't seem to consider it a victory. We walked in heavy silence to a small cottage shielded from the main house by a row of pines.

"You saw the main residence: that's where Amy and

Thomas stay, my family. The boys, too, of course. We have eight of 'em now, and I know the facility was built for ten." He peeked at me. "You seem to know Will from another life, so you can appreciate our need for help."

He unlocked the cottage door, stepped in, but did not turn on the light.

"Shane, my wife and I are the religious type. We've been praying for help for some time without success. Then you showed up with knowledge you should not have, could not have. The Good Book speaks of strangers and angels—"

I held up my hand. "It also mentions devils and demons, so I wouldn't jump to conclusions."

Mr. Loumans flipped on the light and searched my eyes. "I'm a simple man, Shane, and so I will ask directly. Might you be one of them? I have never seen Will respond to a mortal like he responded to you."

I laughed aloud, my shock turning it to a chuckle, then finally trailing off completely. I stared at Mr. L.

"You think I'm an angel."

"I think the possibility exists."

I was dumbfounded. I'd been called many things but never an angel.

"I ran the background check, as I must in these cases. You do not exist. There has not been a Shane Owen near the Twin Cities metro area for nearly five years, and that Shane being a young girl, now deceased."

I froze. I knew her. I *was* her. My jaw dropped, and I tried to speak. Mr. Loumans face broke into uncontained joy. "I can see my words have hit a mark, and I can't tell you how glad we are that you've come. The boys, as you know, needy one and all. Perhaps the most needy being our own."

Mr. Loumans walked into the small kitchen. "This is his food in here. He sometimes does homework in the cottage." He paused and laughed. "Look at me, telling you what transpires. Forgive me." He gestured around the room. "But I'll have him clean things up."

Mr. Loumans walked toward the door. "I do not know the privacy policy by which you operate, and I can't help feeling I discovered your nature by fortunate happenstance. So even though your presence here would bolster the faith of my son, I will keep it under wraps, except to Amy, of course." He winked. "And of course we can overlook the 'failed' background check."

"We're still on the angel thing?" I lifted up a finger, but I had no words. It was the dumbest thing I'd ever heard. Well, aside from a soul-mind inhabiting a thirteen-year-old girl and an eighteen-year-old guy, and being sent back in time by the embodiment of Mrs. Butterworth's syrup bottle while the real soul sleeps next to the Lifeless vegetable of its former body.

Next to that, being an angel sounded rather tame.

Mr. Loumans slipped out into night.

I puffed out air and wandered over to the fridge, opened

it, and stared. It felt right standing there, looking inside.

Must be a guy thing.

"Nothing." I moved to the cupboard. Thirty, maybe forty cans of tuna. "Do angels like tuna?" I smirked, and then frowned. "Does Shane like tuna?" I reached for a can and rummaged through the drawers. I found an opener, removed the lid, and winced.

"Okay, that reeks." I rushed the can out the door and whipped it down the path.

"Dang!"

A kid rounded the corner clutching his head. He reached the steps. "Move over, I need ice."

I stepped back and he pushed through, flew into the kitchen, then soon plopped onto the La-Z-Boy, a ziplock bag of ice resting on his head.

"I came out to say hello." He grimaced. "I didn't know you had a tuna vendetta."

I eased down on the coach across from him. "Sorry 'bout that. Stuff is out to get me."

He switched hands on the ice pack. "I'll get it out of here. It's mine. I'm Thomas, by the way. I'd shake your hand but—"

"Mr. Loumans's son. Good to meet you. He said you came out here on occasion."

"He's being generous. I live out here. It's a zoo in there." He winced and set down the ice pack. "How's it look?"

"Beside the blood spattered across the forehead?"

"Yeah," he chuckled. "Other than that."

"Don't suppose your mother will disown you."

The feelings, they were mine: Crow's. But the words. They came out different. Something male controlled the meter of my words, the tempo of my tongue. I could think girl. But I could only speak guy.

"I don't know what you told Dad out here, but he was sure excited when he got back to the house." Thomas shook his head. "He grabbed Mom and went into the back room, and she screamed. A good scream, you know? Then she *whooshed* me out to say hello."

"And I tuna'd you in the forehead."

He was quiet.

Do guys chat? Do they just sit? This one couldn't handle it.

"So what's my job?" I asked. "What exactly do I do?"

Thomas touched his bluish bump and exhaled. "You'll go to school with the guys. Central High. We all go there. You'll have a cubicle in the guidance office. The idea is that you'll be a liaison between the school and the guys and my dad— and the police."

"So . . .I babysit grown boys and squeal on everyone."

"Yeah, that's pretty much it."

"And get paid in tuna fish."

"No." Thomas set down the ice. "The pay and the job,

they're not so bad. The guys are crazy." He quieted.

"And Will. He's the worst of them, right?"

Thomas shrugged. "You know, a guy lives on the streets for a few years, I guess a reputation follows him, but . . ." He shook his head. "I've lived with him now for a time, and he's not what you think. The guy's room is filled with books, books with titles I can't pronounce. Outside, with the others, yeah, he can be a pain, but alone he's actually pretty quiet."

I frowned. "A pretty quiet thief, and least judging from the phone incident."

"Maybe. Except Dad had three hundred dollars in a clip beneath his phone. Will didn't touch that. What kind of thief takes a phone and leaves three hundred in cash?"

I didn't have an answer.

"Whatever he is," Thomas said, "the girls, they follow him everywhere."

I shifted forward. "They do, huh? Do you know an Adele Raine?"

Thomas rolled his eyes. "She's a hard one to miss. Two grades down. Real smart. Real cute. I see Will and her together sometimes. They're an odd couple."

More confirmation that the tiny snowball had fallen off the mountain and was even now growing, gathering strength. It would become an avalanche and crush Crow if it could not be stopped.

It wasn't as if I could see it coming.

The whole Addy/Will thing had taken me by surprise. There certainly was no precedent. In the years following Jude's Mayday attack, Addy busied herself with volunteerism and extracurriculars.

Well, all except for the dating variety.

She had no interest in the multitude of young men who threw themselves at her, and those who did earn a second look were quickly scared off by me.

I didn't mind. Her noninvolvement with everything male made my job easier. Until she returned from the kennel.

"I volunteered at the dog shelter yesterday." Addy grabbed my arm and held me up at the bus stop. The bus rumbled away, and after a few good-byes the others dispersed.

"Yeah. I know. Bet you're good with them."

She shrugged. "There's been a guy there lately, helping out with walking those dogs. His name's Will."

"Okay. There's nothing unusual about that." I shifted. "Is there?"

Addy smiled, and I rolled my eyes.

"Tell me about him."

"I don't know much. I don't know where he lives or much of anything, really. He doesn't say anything about himself. We just talk about those dogs and walk and . . . I don't know,

Crow. There's something stray about him."

"Maybe you should put him down."

Addy laughed. "Crow. It's not bad stray. It's good stray. He doesn't ask for anything. He doesn't expect anything. Will just comes and goes."

I frowned. "And you're just talking about dogs."

Addy threw her arm around my shoulder. "Yeah. So far."

⁓

"Hello?" said Thomas.

I shook my head. "Sorry, what were you saying?"

"I asked how you knew Adele. She's younger than you."

I thought how much to show, how much to hold. "Her sister, Crow. I knew her pretty well, and so Adele was always there, you know?"

Thomas looked at me hard. "What do you mean, you 'knew her'?"

I pushed my hand through my hair and stammered. "You know how it is. Over now."

His jaw dropped. "That's it. All hope is officially gone."

"I'm not tracking here. Hope of what?"

"Nothing." He fisted his armrest. "It's stupid. I was stupid for even thinking . . . forget it."

I hinted a grin, and Thomas whipped the ice at me, missing badly.

"Shut up. Fine. I was hoping you could help me a little.

Crow's tough. You start out on her wrong side, and she'll chew you up. But an older guy like you? Maybe, I thought, if you and I hung out a little at school, she'd notice me, and that might lead to an introduction and—"

"You like her." I couldn't wipe the grin of my face.

"Don't laugh at me, Shane. I've been pissed at myself too long."

I stared at Thomas. Yeah, he'd been there. I remembered him, like a shadow, floating through school in my wake. He showed up in the strangest places but never said a word, and I never learned his name. If I had lived to see my reunion, we would have shown up in different rental cars, pretended we had shared moments, and passed each other by.

It was harder to judge now, but he wasn't a bad-lookin' kid.

"You should say something. Ask her what she thinks about Voltaire. That'll get her going." I paused. "She's not all that tough."

"Easy for you to say. What's really crazy is, I don't even know what I'd do with someone like her. Where do you take her? I'm not looking for anything, you know? When I'm around her, I can't even think."

Oh, man. She would have liked you so much.

Thomas stood up, delicately touched his forehead, and walked toward the door. "If you don't mind my asking, what happened between you two?"

My head thudded back against the wall. "We were together for a while. Then, suddenly, what we had became lifeless."

He thought for a while, and then nodded. "Well, thanks for the tuna." Thomas, like his father, disappeared into the night.

CHAPTER 14

THE THOUGHTS OF C. RAINE

Maybe one day I can have a reunion with myself.
Sebastian Bach

WHAT'S UP WITH SPECIAL ED TRANSPORTATION? You know, those little minivan-sized buses that scream, 'Screwups inside!" They sure don't build up a kid's confidence.

One of those buggers arrived at Hope Home. We'd been waiting. Mr. Loumans saw to it that all were up nice and early. He thought the curb would be a nice spot to introduce me to the boys.

"First and last name for Mr. Shane."

"Eddie Jackson"

"Sean Klaeburne, with an *e*."

"Will."

Mr. Loumans sighed. "Last name, Will."

"Johnson."

"His name is Will Kroft. Next?"

And on they went. Satisfied that we had been properly acquainted, Mr. Loumans then leaned over to me. "Is it appropriate to use some of your unique"—he frowned, and then lightened—"abilities for illustrative purposes?"

"I don't know what you mean. What do you want me to do?"

He cleared his throat. "Now, boys. Listen as Mr. Shane demonstrates what a little attention can do. Shane, will you repeat their names?"

"Eddie Jackson, Sean Klaeburne with an *e* . . ." It wasn't hard. I had gone to school with these idiots for a year. I finished the list, and Mr. Loumans looked to the sky, a heavenly glow on his face. Yes, my memory cemented the deal. I could see it. I was a certified heavenly being, despite my apparent violent nature when it came to cans of tuna fish.

I stepped onto the bus and plunked down in the front seat. I needed to think.

I could keep track of Will at Hope Home, keep him away from Adele, but school was another matter. From a cubicle in the guidance office, how do you keep two students apart?

Thomas huffed up the bus steps, sporting a good shiner.

"Hey, Tommy, where'd you get that beauty?" Eddie pointed. "You do that, Will?"

I whipped around. "I did it."

The bus went silent and stayed that way throughout the drive to school. *There has to be a way to make Addy see Will for what he is. She won't believe me, not in this body. Of course, she might believe Crow.*

Brakes hissed, the door opened, and the kids from Hope Home, so hesitant to enter the bus, pounded down the aisle, ready to wreak havoc on this fine educational institution. They quickly disappeared into the crowd filing toward three sets of double doors.

But not Will. He slithered off the bus, slow and easy, pausing when he reached my seat.

"You don't scare me," Will said.

"Not yet, huh?"

"Not at all." He slapped my shoulder and walked away.

"I'll pop in second hour, Will," I called.

"Sure thing, Mom."

"Speak to Adele before then, and I'll kill you."

He glanced over his shoulder and smirked. I grinned back, though inside I felt he had me beat.

⁓

I walked through Central High. It looked the same—no reason it shouldn't, as I was last there a few weeks ago. But the halls felt tighter, the voices sounded louder.

Girls' laughter sure was.

"Hey, Shane!"

I spun and watched Thomas weave awkwardly between the masses.

Yeah, I remembered him pretty well.

I waited, and he huffed up with his plus-size backpack. "We walk through the same halls, but it's like we're pushing through different schools."

I readjusted his sagging pack across his back. "What d'ya mean?"

"Everyone stares at you. Guys mutter. Girls group together and look. I walk, and nothing." He quickly spun, that backpack slugging me in the shoulder. "Straight in front of you. Do you see her? It's Crow."

Crow stood surrounded by five or six disciples. Gigi, Heidi, Kell, all suck-ups, wanting a piece of Crow's throne. At year's end, she had planned to bestow the mantle of bad girl upon one of the deserving juniors, and there were plenty who wanted a crack at the title.

Though I never did pass the baton, Kell was my final choice.

"What do I do?" Both Thomas and I asked in unison.

"You go talk to her." We said that together, too.

"Listen, Thomas." I grabbed him by the backpack strap and spun him around. "There are things I can tell you about

Crow, things I want to tell you. It will help your cause with her. But believe me, it wouldn't be good for Crow to see *me* right now, so let's walk the other way."

I risked another glance toward the lockers. Crow stared back. Not looked, stared, with tired eyes but a face wild and beautiful. Those around Crow laughed, but her face didn't crack. She was beyond that: she'd seen too much.

Crow appeared amused, as if the bizarre had marched into her domain.

She broke out of her circle, the kids parting, and walked straight at me, stopping square in front, a hair too close for my comfort.

I searched for any evidence that Sadie was right. That my first time back changed me for the better. Crow's clothes were the same: black top and black jeans. Crow's cold sensuality, still my desired vibe.

But it clicked. She came toward me. I had never lowered myself to that. Was she hard? Yeah, the years had taken their toll. But my arrogant pride had taken a hit.

A very good development.

"I've not seen you here before," Crow said.

"I've not been here before."

She squinted and let her unblinking eyes search mine, and when she spoke, her words were soft, reaching, "But I know you. Or you know me. Or something. Is that right?"

I raised my eyebrows and exhaled slowly, drawn to the gentleness in me. "If so, let's make a new start. I'll go first. My name's Shane." My hand extended, and she peeked at it, made no move to grasp it.

Her face twitched. "Your last name?"

"My last name is Owen. And you are?"

Crow's legs buckled and she stumbled backward, her fair skin blanching still further. Her head shook in little spasms, and for a second I thought she was having a seizure. She steadied herself, grinned, lifted a finger and waggled it in my face. "Very good. Who have you been speaking to? Basil? No, Mel. Not Addy. She wouldn't mess with that."

"I just told you my name, Crow. That's all."

"You know my name. You know just what to say," she whispered.

Dong. The obnoxious first bell rang. She buried her finger in my chest, twisted it, and flicked up, nicking my chin. "I'll see you around, Shane Owen."

"I hope so."

Kids scurried after her. Except for Thomas.

"Okay, that was weird. That looked like a relationship that, number one, is not over, and number two, never started."

"You, uh . . ." I winced. "You may have nailed it there, friend. I'll explain more later." I slapped his shoulder and headed for the guidance office, my body shaking.

Who knew that coming face-to-face with yourself could be so terrifying?

—

"Shane Owen? Oh, welcome to Central!" Ms. Crebat, our overly jubilant guidance counselor, led me past the inspirational posters to a small cubicle in the back of the room. "I know it's small, but you're working with only eight kids." She clapped her hands together. "You know, maybe you could be convinced to help with some of our other needy students as well. When you have time, of course."

I shrugged. "Yeah, no problem."

"Oh, how wonderful!" She grabbed both my hands and squeezed. "If there's anything you need."

"Just these schedules." I handed her the list. Her eyes glossed over.

"Will Kroft is easy. ISS. In-school suspension." Ms. Crebat glanced to her left and her right, and then lowered her voice. "It's not right, you know."

"I don't follow."

She took another look around the office. "What they do to that young man. That boy of yours was a marked kid when he arrived. Would you believe an officer called the entire staff together on Will's first day? He told us there was no cause for concern, but that violence seemed to accompany our new student. I asked him if he had seen Will being violent. He said no, but the seed was sown." Ms. Crebat exhaled. "That first morning I sat down and talked with Will for nearly an hour. Charming kid. Likable kid. If it wasn't for that officer, he would have had a chance here. But by afternoon he was ISS. I think some believe he single-handedly accounts for every problem in this school.

"I'll get you the other schedules right away." She scuttled out of the room, and I eased down into my roller chair.

"Two," I whispered. "That makes two." Yesterday, Thomas, and now Ms. Crebat, both of them defending the undefendable. But I'd heard it myself: "Down by the river . . . a girl about my age, and I don't think she's going to make it." It's hard to believe he was an innocent bystander.

Of course, I also saw Will turn down a warm bed and help an old man into a police truck.

My old life was getting murkier.

I pushed back and rolled toward the wall.

There. I stared into the empty cubicle near the door and remembered Crow's one guidance office visit. The scene of her, of my, greatest embarrassment.

That morning with Basil. Let's stop that while I'm here.

CHAPTER 15

THE THOUGHTS OF C. RAINE

An alliance with a powerful person is never safe.

Phaedrus

I QUIETLY OPENED THE DOOR INTO ROOM 56. ISS. Every attempt had been made to turn this place into a maximum-security prison. Windows? Cinder block sealed and, like the office, painted powder blue, the color designed to perpetuate mental instability.

Flies buzzed the fluorescent lights, and the stale smell of vomit permeated the place.

Seven carrels graced the perimeter of the room, all facing out, positioned to prevent any view of humanity. In the center of the room, two desks fronted two paras who stared blankly into the abyss. They were victims of the room as well. The carpet was brown, stained with large spots of unknown fluid.

My former-life stays in ISS depressed me enough that even I retreated when a threat was given. Today, only Will was in prison, and when I opened the door, he was whistling.

Happy sounds were not allowed in ISS.

A para pounded her desk. "Will, shut the mouth now, or we can help with the process."

Was that a threat? Sure. But within the walls of Room 56, different laws applied. It was similar to speeding on the Indian reservation. Get pulled over and you never knew what to expect.

Large Marge, as we called her, rose to her feet. She was nearly as wide as she was tall, and when she stood, her considerable girth knocked books and papers clean off her desk. This time the entire desk lifted and fell with a thump. "I said, 'Stop whistling'!"

"I can't, Large Marge. I'm in a good mood." Will did not turn. "I've got me a date. Ever had one of those? I can explain how they work, if you like." He cranked his head around and saw me in the doorway. "The Prophet. Come on in. I think we have some empty chairs."

"How's the prisoner?" I winked at Marge, and she blushed and flattened her hair.

"He's unusually happy today. You must be Shane."

"Mr. Shane, the Prophet." Will started whistling again. I walked over to the carrel on his left and pulled its chair next to his.

He rocked back and forth. "Mm-mm. Smell that stagnant air? This is what I get to experience. Probably much different than your education."

"You'd be surprised." I grabbed the front leg of his chair and shoved it back down to earth. Behind me, women sighed with delight at the show of strength. "Sounds like you got a date."

He nodded big, and a crease of pleasure worked across his face. Yeah, there was something magnetic about him. Will and Basil, they both had it. Poor Thomas.

"Now," I continued, "you can't leave the grounds for dates. Mr. L was pretty clear on this point."

"You're right, Wise One." He pointed to his temple, created two upturned okay signs with his hands, and hummed. "So I will go on a date in my mind."

"A mental date."

"A mental date," he repeated. "Yeah, that's all I'm allowed, but as you see, I've learned to be satisfied with little things."

"And following your mental date," I bent over and whispered, "might you just call 555-0177?"

His hands opened. He peeked at me and licked his lips.

"And after you 'borrow' a car, you might drive, lights off, to 7934 Sycamore Circle, yes? Four raps on the back window. And then it's a crapshoot. Who is going to open the shade? It could be Adele. Ah, the joy if that happens, because your mental date turns into reality." I leaned in even closer. "Or it might be Crow, in which case your date will take a painful turn."

Will jumped to his feet, tripped on his chair, and staggered back against a wall. "I don't know who you are, but—"

"No, you don't. But you'll be canceling that date, or when you open the shade, it'll be me you'll see." I approached him and lowered my voice. "And I know where Jude keeps the gun. Are we clear?" I gestured toward his fallen chair. He eased over, picked it up, and plunked down in it.

"We're clear," he whispered.

I turned to Large Marge. "I don't think you'll have any more whistling issues." I closed the door on Will's curse, and exhaled hard.

My threats held no bite, all my words just so much hot air. The truth was that pacifist Jude owned no gun, and I surely wouldn't be able to intercept every date. I needed a more permanent solution. Basil wasn't the answer, but I sure needed help.

I needed Crow.

I spent the rest of the day in the photographic darkroom, my favorite room in which to cut class. The digital revolution pushed the room into disuse. It sat—small, abandoned, forgotten—near the art room, deep in the bowels of the school.

Pitch-black. Unused. A perfect place to steal a nap.

I never told my disciples about the hiding place. I never told Mel. Only Basil was privy to my hideaways, and he'd peek into the darkroom from time to time.

It was there I first felt it strong. Sitting by Basil in the dark, my head on his shoulder. The switch happened. He must have felt it, too, though now I see how much earlier his mind had navigated the forbidden. We kissed. And I pulled away and elbowed him in the gut. Yes, to hurt him, but more to remind myself of the danger.

But the worst part of the deal was that throughout and beyond the kiss, I never gave his girlfriend Mel a thought. Of course, if the roles had been reversed, Mel would have rejoiced in victory.

Sitting in the darkroom as Shane, unaware of Crow's thoughts and plans, frustrated me to no end. What were the odds that she'd show up on this day? By the end of seventh hour, I'd given up. I stood and stretched and exited the room. I let my eyes adjust and marched slowly back toward the guidance office. The last bell rang. Halls filled and then emptied, but I made no move for the buses. My first day at work reminded me of Will's strength, and threatening him into submission would work for only so long.

Inside my cubicle, I shuffled some schedules, stared around the empty room, and wandered to the door. I flicked off the light and stepped into the hall.

"You're not the first Shane Owen I've known."

The guidance door latched behind me with a loud click. Across the hall, Crow leaned back, fingers wriggling into her pockets. Her eyes rested heavily on me, and my palms sweated.

"It's a common name around here?" I asked.

"No."

The school had cleared out, except for a few straggling teachers. The roar of a distant bus fell silent, and Central felt empty, as did I.

"Shane Owen showed up during middle school, popped into my old tree house. In a few weeks she became my best friend, my soul mate. She stayed right up until my worst day, and then she vanished, as though she'd never been here at all. A storm took her." Crow paused. "She knew stuff; she just knew stuff."

This wasn't typical Crow. Not at all. I never offered my past to a stranger. But that was the difference—I was no stranger. She was speaking to her own soul, and her defenses dropped.

So did mine.

"A storm took her." I shifted my weight on weakening legs and forced a grin. "It just blew her out to sea, I'll bet."

"Yeah," Crow squinted. "On a raft."

"A bouncy raft," I said, and gave my head a shake. "That's

quite a story. Anyone ever find her?" I backed against the opposite wall, buried my hands in my pockets, and fingered the locket. She would freak.

"I don't know. Do you?"

"How would I know about a girl you met years ago?"

She shrugged and swept back her hair.

Wow, was I gorgeous.

Crow rubbed the scar on her forearm. "How does anybody know anything?"

We gazed at each other for a minute or more. A thinking gaze. A figuring gaze. "I need to get back." I cleared my throat. "Missed the bus, and it'll be a long walk."

"Where do you live, Shane?"

"Hope Home. I took a job there."

Her lips curled, and she spoke so quietly I barely heard. "Will lives with you."

"Adele lives with you."

Crow stiffened. "What do you care about Addy?"

There probably was a better way to do this, but I couldn't think of it. "Listen, I'm in the middle of a predicament, and I need to know about Will and Adele. It's part of my job. How close are they? I mean, how far gone is she?"

Crow rocked, looked off into the distance, and her face hardened. "She says she loves him."

I breathed heavily. "Crow, due to my peculiar position,

one that I am not at liberty to discuss right now, I have a vested interest in seeing that they *not* end up as a couple. How do you feel about that?"

"Keep talking."

"As I recall, you also share that sentiment."

"As you recall? Who have you been talking to—"

I waved her off. "I'll have better luck destroying this relationship if I can get your assistance. Any interest?"

Crow thought for a while. "You won't touch her. You never will. So if this is an attempt to open the door for yourself, I have nothing to say to you except, Watch your back."

"No!" I exhaled. "No, I don't want anything from her."

Crow was silent, trying, it seemed, to figure out why she felt so comfortable with me. She peeked up. "He's all wrong for her."

I shrugged. "Yeah, he is."

"But I told her I wouldn't interfere. I've done that too many times already."

The list of guys I deemed not good enough had been extensive, and my protective streak ran deep and fierce. Addy had sucked from me a promise to stay out of her love life. I reluctantly agreed.

Crow would never go back on Adele.

"Yeah, I know I— you did." I straightened and took a few steps toward her. "So I won't ask you to do anything. Just help me. I'll take it on. I'll do it, work on it from Will's end. All I need is a complete history of what's happened between them so far. Anything you know about him. I need his story."

"You want me to write it down?" Crow slowly pushed off the wall and approached. She circled me, stopping directly in front. "Yeah, I'll do that."

"Okay, well then, I need to be going." I grabbed her by the arm and looked into her eyes. Confused eyes. "Crow, you're beautiful."

"I know." Her face hardened. "So are you."

I grinned. She didn't.

"Crow! Where the he—" Basil huffed up the hall and skidded to a halt beside her. My hand was still on her arm, and Basil reached out and pried loose my fingers. "I'm surprised you still have all your digits. . . . I know you."

"Hey, Shane!" Thomas ran up from the other direction. "You missed the bus."

The four of us stood, gawking at one another. Basil's lips slowly parted. "You're the jerk who watched my sled get tagged."

"You're the pizza sign who got thrashed by an eggplant." I turned to Thomas, rounded his shoulder with one arm, and pulled him nearer. "Crow, Basil, this is Thomas; his parents run Hope Home, so he's my boss."

Thomas raised his hands. "I'm not really his boss—"

"How do you know my name?" Basil frowned, his eyes slits. "Crow, did you tell him?"

She rolled her eyes. "Let it go, Basil. There's something unnatural going on. You push him, and I don't think it'll be pretty." Crow turned back toward me, a slight smile tugging at her lips.

"I think he needs to be pushed," Basil said.

I stepped toward him. "How's Dove? Bet she's looking forward to her gardens come spring. And your dad? I saw him and another officer when I first got to town."

Basil glanced at Crow. "Did you tell—"

"Told ya." Crow's face held panic, and she backed away. "I'd like you to meet Shane Owen."

Thomas swallowed hard. "I'm more the son of his boss, but still. So Crow, I've uh, I've been meaning to ask—"

"Shane Owen. Shane Owen, I know that name . . . crap." Basil winced. "You ain't her, though."

Crow backhanded Basil hard. "But you wish he was." She turned and stomped away. Basil scurried after her, paused to glance at me over his shoulder, and then rounded the corner.

Thomas and I stood in silence.

"Hi Crow, how nice to meet you. Me? Oh, I wanted to see if you'd like to grab a coffee. I'm headed that way. My name? Thomas Loumans. But I realize it's hard to care about that with *Shane* around." He shoved me. "Maybe just stop introducing me. I felt less invisible when you weren't here."

CHAPTER 16

THE THOUGHTS OF C. RAINE

Pity is for the living, envy is for the dead.
Mark Twain

I WALKED DOWN THE SNOWY ROAD, THOMAS SILENT AT MY SIDE.
It's true I hadn't done much for his cause, which might, in retrospect, have been a tremendous miscalculation. There is a fantastic, stabilizing effect when a level-headed guy likes you. It's like taking a seasickness pill. The waves don't seem so big, and though you still get sick, it seems to get cleaned up quicker.

I would have liked to tell Thomas my story. I think he might have believed it, or half believed it. I could sure accompany it with much convincing proof. But my tasks were complicated, and I remained silent, listening to the crunch of my feet and the rumble of traffic.

And one oncoming snowmobile.

Basil roared up to us and swished me with snow. He lifted his visor and massaged the pressure mark. "Get on!"

Thomas started toward the sled.

"Not you!" Basil pointed. "You." He scooted forward, and I peeked at Thomas, raised my eyebrows.

"Oh, go ahead." Thomas swept snow off his jeans. "Forget that I waited for you."

I tongued my cheek and turned to Basil. "You're driving me home?"

"Nope. Get on."

"One short ride."

A half hour later we reached Basil's corner of Hennepin, and Basil eased to the snow mound that hid the curb.

We walked by Basil's apartment toward Lake Calhoun. We rounded the lake, enjoying an extremely awkward half hour of silence, and veered onto Lake Harriet Parkway. Basil headed for the band shell. There, on the stage, he plunked down. "Sit."

He looked to be sinking into another quiet phase, but I'd had enough.

"I don't mean to mess with this little drama, but I actually work, and I need to get back, so tell me—"

"Do you know what happened here ten years ago? I was eight?"

"You met Crow for the first time. She was sitting right there." I pointed to the back bench. "You were across the aisle there. She was cute, but you were only eight. You waved, and she didn't, and something beautiful started.

"But then a few years later, Shane showed up, and it turned out there was a lot less to you than Crow thought. Anything else you want to say?"

Basil jumped up. "So that's what she told you, huh? Even now, my mom lets her stay at her place 'cause at home, Crow has nothing! She's a head case. A freakin' hot head case, but she's *my* head case, you got that? Crow is mine."

Paying for lunch had morphed into full-blown ownership. Frightening. Basil was sweet and kind and giving. He was also the friend from Hades. Interestingly, the two can coexist.

"I see. So what about Mel? Crow mentioned you spend quite a bit of time together. Mel's all fine with this pimping side?"

Basil's mouth hung open. I'm sure his goal had been to bring me onto his home turf and lay down the law. Nothing went the way he planned. Typical Basil.

"Mel knows what she needs to know," he said quietly.

I stood. "Isn't she your girlfriend?"

"She's what I want her to be."

Inside my chest floated a steamy anger, like someone had popped the top of a pressure valve.

"I'm taking Crow from you." I shoved Basil back onto the stage and walked away. "You never had her. You never will."

"I'll prove it! When I'm done, you'll see," he shouted. It

was no idle threat. He would try to prove it. I knew where, and I knew when. For the first time I felt worry—not for Addy, but for Crow.

For me.

I broke into a slow jog—I had a ways to go. "Protect Addy from Will. Protect Crow from Basil." My steps fell to the rhythm of the mantra.

Preventing Mayday was becoming more and more challenging.

———

Three hours later, I stood in front of Mom's place, Basil's words ringing in my head.

"Crow!" I pounded on her window. "You in there?"

The curtain shifted, and her voice reached into the night. "In front."

I marched onto the driveway and waited beneath the streetlamp's glow. The front door swung open. Crow stepped into the chill, wearing only an oversize black T-shirt. I exhaled and tried to look away, but I couldn't. She motioned me nearer, and I obeyed.

"You stalking me now?" She took a step closer. "That's not nearly as appealing as the mysterious vibe you were working."

"I know." I bent over and packed a tight snowball, let it fall to the ground. "I want to talk."

"Not inside," she said.

"You said you had a tree house?"

She thought hard. "Yeah. Okay." The door closed, and when Crow reappeared, she was wrapped in a blanket, her bare legs stuffed into winter boots. Stinking adorable.

I trudged through the snow and climbed the steps, squeezed through the hole. I barely fit. Crow followed, reached the top, and shivered. She scooted near me, and my body tingled. We were in frightening territory.

I turned and faced her. "There's stuff I want to tell you."

She reached behind a stack of books, grabbed a cigarette, lit it, took a drag, and offered it to me.

I never had cigarettes up here before. More changes to Crow's life.

I stared at Crow's outstretched hand. *Does this Shane smoke?*

Four big hacks.

Nope.

I handed it back.

"Do you believe in reincarnation, Shane?"

I chuckled. "I used to. I read a lot of Hindu writs, and they almost had me convinced, but my experience says otherwise."

"One fifth of the world does," Crow said. "And if they're wrong, you have a lot of explaining to do."

For once, I was in no mood to talk philosophy. "We need to talk about Basil. The guy is slimy. I just spoke with him."

"Basil is a lot of things." Crow picked at the floorboards. "He's a hard-luck case."

"No. He knows exactly what he's doing."

"And what is he doing?"

"He'll expect a gift this Christmas. Something you don't want to give him. You know it; I know you do. I remember thinking, feeling it when Basil and I were together. Do you know what I mean?"

Crow tossed the cigarette and ground the butt into the floor. "What the hell? When Basil and you were together?" She paused. "There is not one explanation in any of these books that explains your possessing the facts you do. Please, is there something I need to know?"

"Yeah," I swallowed. "But I can't go there right now. I need you to focus. I'm worried. For you."

Crow rubbed her arms. "You've just joined a very small club. Listen, Basil's doing fine. He has Mel. Good for them both."

"But as far as he's concerned, you're the challenge, the one always there but just out of reach," I said. "I'm telling you so you're ready. So when the time comes, you're alert, and your head's on straight."

"Caution noted. I consider myself warned." Crow peeked into my eyes. "And what do you want from me?" She raised her black fingernails to her mouth.

"Don't tell her, child."

Sadie sat, cross-legged, knitting needles in hand. She touched my neck. "I go to all this work makin' you a scarf, and you don't even wear it."

I point at Sadie. Crow doesn't turn. "I'm waiting. You tell me all about Basil, but you can't say anything about yourself? What's with that?"

"Shane, she can't see me. And I'm only interrupting as you be messin' with the system again. Too much information goin' out to too many people. The future is changing because of you, and not in ways you want it to. People are making decisions based on info they should not yet have."

"Where are you, Shane?" Crow waved her hand in front of my face. I forced a smile in her direction and turned back to Sadie.

"So listen," Sadie said. "This is not a request. Consider it commanded. No more prophesying. No more of that. Tellin' folks what they done in private and warning them of what's to come. Your own future is hanging close as is. The locket, take a look."

I'd forgotten about the colors. I forced my fingers into my pocket and pulled out the chain. I slowly opened the clasp. Yellow had turned to brilliant orange. Red was coming. I'd dreamed red enough to know. Red meant death.

Time was running out.

Crow pushed back. "Where did you get that? What's going on?"

I glanced from Crow to Sadie to Crow to nobody. I pocketed my locket. "Nothing. I need to go."

"Listen." Crow sounded near desperate. I'd never heard the tone. "Would you ever consider coming with me to Christmas? I can't bear it here without somebody. Normally, Addy and I stagger through the holiday together, but this year she'll be occupied."

I thought on that, watched fear ripple across Crow's face. She leaned forward and let the blanket fall, slipped into my arms, and pulled them tight around her. My body tingled, warmed, hardened.

Crow shifted inside my hold; the unbreakable Crow felt soft, open, and she pressed her nose into my neck. I knew if her lips reached mine, something both sensual and really strange wouldn't be far behind. We were already one, soul mates in the truest sense. Like half of a magnet, my soul was drawn, desperate to enter the body it had inhabited. But more than my soul. This body, this Shane, burned with an aggression I'd never felt. I wanted Crow, all of her.

I forced my body back, gently held her face, and kissed her . . . on the forehead, and on both cheeks.

"Yes, Crow. I want to be where you are." I reached for the blanket and wrapped it around her shoulders, paused, and watched her open her eyes.

"I've never met anybody like you," she whispered.

"Yeah, you have."

Crow thought for a moment. "Good. Well, good." She rubbed her face and reached for another cigarette. "Adele is bringing someone, too."

I froze. Addy hadn't brought anyone the last time through.

"Then I'll definitely be here."

CHAPTER 17

THE THOUGHTS OF C. RAINE

They must often change, who would be
constant in happiness or wisdom.
Confucius

I RAN AWAY FROM HOME THE LAST DAY OF MY JUNIOR YEAR.
Jude had taken a three-month teaching position in some
teach-a-shrink program, and, tired of enduring Mom's
wrath, and with no desire to return to another summer's
incarceration at the minimum-wage Shack, it seemed a
good time to bail. I told Basil and Mel that I'd be in touch,
and hopped the light rail directly from school, ending at
the twisty, tangled mess that was the downtown St. Paul
train depot.

It wasn't as easy as I figured. Coal cars ruled the day, and
I didn't find the thought of riding high on a mound of soot
particularly appealing. But eventually, Burlington Northern
hauled out of the way, and a Canadian line snaked onto

the tracks. Filled with empty boxcars, it was the perfect transport.

I threw my pack inside. Heavy thing, it held six books, including the writings of Confucius, the Dalai Lama, the Holy Bible, a translation of the Quran, and some Indian New Age writs—I was passing through a spiritual phase— two candles, incense, and matches. Five PowerBars, an iPad, some personals, and my knife bulged that pack to the breaking point. I nestled back, folded my hands behind my head, and sighed.

"Crow? Crow! Where are you?"

"Addy?"

It turned out Basil had cracked and told Addy, whose desperate call was plenty loud to alert railmen of my escape.

I stuck my head out the open side of the boxcar. "Over here. You should be home. I'm kind of busy at the moment."

"Maybe . . ." She glanced around the depot, at the tracks, into the boxcar. Nerves set her leg bouncing. "Maybe I should go with you?"

Can't you just hear that conviction?

Have you ever been loved for no reason? Have you ever felt so despicable that the presence of a kind soul makes you feel even more heinous? I did, but this was Adele, and I could never turn her down. Why tell you all this?

On that day, I taught my sister how to jump a train. It

took her some effort. She was fighting conscience throughout the maneuver, and received several bruises for her hesitation, but eventually she got it. I thought the Canadian would take us north. We ended up in Chicago, where Addy offered a sigh so doleful, we switched trains and headed back home.

The point is, Addy had experience jumping trains.

Something to keep in mind.

⁓

Christmastime at Hope Home was a festive affair.

Do four Christmas trees seem excessive to you? How about a life-size manger scene in the front yard, complete with twenty-four wooden figurines, at least a dozen more than actually appeared in the biblical narrative? And what would you say to Christmas music, streaming twenty-four/seven from a speaker hung from a large elm?

Yep. That's what I said.

And lights. There are Christmas lighters, and Christmas leeches: people who suck enjoyment from the lighters' overdone efforts.

Mr. Loumans was a lighter and went all in.

Racing around the roof of the three-story, he hung icicle lights and bulb lights and flashers. The sheer quantity was oppressive, the variety visually assaulting, but somehow at night it all worked.

But for all the excitement going on outside, the inside of his place was, by his report, a morgue—a pleasant morgue.

"Your influence on Will has been nothing short of miraculous." He smirked down at me from the top of the ladder.

"Miraculous, huh? That might be overstated." I winced, unraveled a vicious knot in a string of lights, and fed him more slack. He apparently felt it his duty to rival the moon with Christmas lights.

"I think not. I need to tell you this. The boy had a perfect week, which, in turn, meant the rest of the boys had perfect weeks."

"Great for you, and Ms. Amy, and Thomas." I stared at the pile of dead flashers heaped in the snow. "You all deserve a little peace on earth. So tell me about Christmas at Hope Home. Will the boys go somewhere?"

"All but Will." Mr. Loumans paused. "Surely you have been long monitoring his unique case, so I'll spare you the details. The thing is . . ." He lowered a string of lights and stepped onto the top rung. "Will has received an invitation. I spoke to the host family. I've half a mind to let him go."

"And the other half?"

"Thinks it a recipe for disaster. I thought I'd consult with you. Any thoughts?"

"I take it we're talking about a friend from school?"

Mr. Loumans climbed down and clapped ice from his gloves. "That should do it." He turned to me. "Yeah. A girl." He looked over his illuminated creation. "Have I reason for concern?"

I exhaled. Given my angelic constitution, I could've, with one sentence, one word from the Lord, swayed the man and prevented any Christmas chaos. Why I didn't still mystifies, as it might have made all the difference. But the mind of man is confusing beyond measure.

"Here's what you do. Let him go. But to be safe, give me free rein on Christmas Eve as well. I'll check in on Will from time to time."

Mr. Loumans stepped forward and placed his left hand on my right shoulder. He squeezed. A strong, man squeeze. An I-trust-you-with-this squeeze. Had he been my dad, I knew one thing: no matter how loudly I had screamed, no matter how hard Jude had tried to force him out, he would never have left.

"Okay. I believe in you."

Mr. L spoke the words—I know it, I saw his lips move. But inside my brain, the voice I heard was Dad's. How this happened, I cannot explain. I can only record the impact.

It had been thirteen years since Dad spoke those words at my piano recital. But there beside Mr. L, a wash of longing surged over me, and I wanted nothing more than to see my father's face.

The really scary part? I wanted to see him more than Addy.

I broke free from Mr. L's grasp and ran.

I sprinted up the lane to my cottage, opened the door, and slammed it before I busted. Tears fell free; I made no effort to stop them.

But it wasn't Shane. Yeah, he throated the sounds, bawling awkward and ugly, but these were deep-down tears, bubbling up from wherever I was inside that body. They were my tears because no man with strength had ever touched me or anyone else I knew without wanting something back. Mr. Loumans's hand was gentle and honest and powerful, and I wondered where Dad was now. Was he alive? Remarried? Would he be alone this Christmas?

I plunked onto the chair and forced my hand through my hair.

"Can't get sidetracked here. I got a job to do and a sister to protect—"

"Whoa. Rough Christmas, huh?"

I leaped up. Will sat in the corner, his eyes sparkling.

"How did you get in here?" I rubbed my eyes with the heels of my hands.

"Relax, Prophet. I didn't take your cell phone or anything." He grinned. "I even knocked. Your door was unlocked and it was cold, so I thought I'd sit inside. I've been waiting ISS proper. I came to make peace."

"You want peace?"

"Well, actually, I don't care what you think of me. I'm interested in seeing Adele, and it's seemin' like I need to go through you to do that."

I stared at him. There was no posturing. He was just a kid.

He continued. "I've put up a perfect week. Did Mr. L tell you that? I have an invite to Adele's house on Christmas Eve. I want to go. Is that so bad?"

"No. Not so bad."

He shifted in his seat. "Adele's a great girl."

"Yeah, she is."

"So what do you have against the two of us—I mean, it ain't normal. You show up dead-on that I can't see her, can't talk to her, or you're going to kill me? That's not 'beat the crap out of me,' that's 'kill me.' Who threatens someone over a date? Something's wrong with that." He looked around the cottage and raised his arms. "I know I ain't perfect. Not even close. But your hating on her and me is over the top. You're keeping something. Would you care if I wanted to see someone else?"

"No."

"You care only about Adele."

"Yes."

His eyes narrowed. "Why?"

Sadie's warning floated in, floated out. "I don't know." I paused. "You can save your words. I talked to Mr. Loumans. I told him that he should let you go. Pay me later."

Will jumped to his feet. "Shut up!"

I said nothing.

"For real? The talk-to-her-and-I'll-kill-you guy pulled a one eighty? What the heck?" Will cast me a sideways glance and walked up to me. "You ain't so bad, Prophet."

"Do yourself a favor. Try to speak in complete sentences. Crow likes that."

"Yeah, okay." He walked toward the door and paused. "Merry Christmas, Mr. Shane."

"Merry Christmas, Will."

He whistled and pushed out into the cold.

Maybe choice is overrated. How could it be that the one relationship I came back to destroy, I was now allowing? What happened? Was it seeing Crow's fear, feeling her body, experiencing the touch of a father figure? Why was my mind fixed more on Crow than Adele? Something greater than self-preservation was at work. Call it fate, or providence, but some things might be hardwired into the historical record.

The Dalai Lama would have a hard time with that one.

CHAPTER 18

THE THOUGHTS OF C. RAINE

When evil men plot, good men must plan.
Martin Luther King Jr.

I ARRIVED AT SCHOOL TO A CRYING MEL. Not light sobs. Large, heaving noises that sounded two parts animal, one part girl. A ring of friends pinned her against a locker and, by all appearances, did their best to console her, several of them wiping tears from their own eyes. The hall looked like a disaster triage.

I pushed my way nearer. No, I had not planned on offering condolences. That would've ended with my speaking of slimy Basil and revealing more to Mel than I felt comfortable with, since Sadie's drive-by. But she was one of my former best friends, so I felt some responsibility. I couldn't recall Mel ever being so distraught.

Ever.

"Shane!" Mel screamed and broke out of her circle. She grasped onto me, her nails making painful inroads into my arms. She looked to me wide-eyed, choking back those noises.

"Do I know you?" I paused and let my lie take root, then continued. "Whatever's going on, I'm sure it'll all work out, you know?"

"We need to talk." Mel yanked me away from the guidance office and down the main hall. Students parted in front of her despair, and we quickly reached the choir room. She glanced both ways, rushed me through the door and into a practice room. She quietly shut the door; lights automatically flashed on, and more tears fell. Five minutes later, Mel had composed herself and related her tale of woe.

I would not make it to the guidance office that day.

———

Mel sang in the choir; most days this was a fact of little consequence other than that she possessed a general knowledge of when the practice rooms were unoccupied. This provided her and Basil a cozy place to get serious within the confines of the school, but I digress . . . though not much.

She arrived early this morning to help prepare for the Christmas—I'm sorry, *Winter*—choir concert. Mel was on choir-robe detail. The sheet on the rack listed the garments' sizes, from "petite" to "grande." The entire choir had, the previous day, lined up, skinniest to fattest, in a rare acknowledgment of the truth, in order to receive their robe assignments. After all, those black tents with Big Bird yellow collars must fit properly.

After the school's robes had been matched with appropriately—or inappropriately—sized singers, a master list was created. Petite Kelli Hawthorne would model robe number 1, and so on, right up to grande Lionel Ferrar, dashing in robe number 98. The list of names and numbers was posted in preparation for the concert, and the robes were returned to their hangers. Mel arrived early in the morning to assure that, come concert time, the robes would be found hanging in proper numerical order.

After a few perfunctory checks, Mel was satisfied, and turned to leave. And paused.

Why she bothered to check the master list, she couldn't say. How different for us all had she not.

But she did. Kelli Hawthorne, number 1. David Teasel number 2. David starting-forward-on-the-basketball-team Teasel was number 2? She went on, chuckling, thinking about the miniskirt robe he would sport until she reached Lionel Ferrar at number 5. His powerful tenor scraped the boundaries of each doorframe he entered. Lionel was number 5? The list had been doctored.

"So I asked myself, Who would have done it? Who would want to cause that much chaos before a concert? Who has something against Mr. Grion?"

I lifted my palms.

"Only one person. Someone booted from the choir." She nodded big and slow.

"Basil," I whispered.

"He told you about that?" Mel frowned.

"No, I just heard it in passing."

Mel came to the same conclusion I did. She set out in search of Basil, not so much angry as amused. She wanted to ask him if she should ignore the messed-up list. After all, robes were her responsibility, not assignments.

She checked the places where Basil could get his hands on a computer and printer, where he could have created a deliciously insidious alternative posting, but the media center, computer lab, and business center were still locked down. On a lark, she tried the guidance office. The door swung open and the light was on, and there's where, sitting in the choir's practice room, I almost threw up. I swallowed the burn and methodically thumped my forehead with the heel of my hand.

"You okay?" Mel asked.

I stopped thumping and squeezed the bridge of my nose. "Keep going."

Mel stepped inside the guidance office. Right around the corner, on the floor, her body curled up inside an empty cubicle, slept Crow, a notebook fallen from her hands.

"She didn't wake up when the door opened?" I asked, knowing the tragic answer.

"It's a very quiet door."

I hate quiet doors.

Mel was more than a little curious and tiptoed over to Crow, who had spent some time on herself.

"Shane, she wasn't even wearing black."

I said nothing, and Mel continued.

Curiosity got the best of her, and she bent down on one knee and opened the notebook.

Shane,

Here is what I know. I spent last night pulling it all together. I did it for you.

"Honest, that's where I stopped." It didn't matter, and I gestured for the rest with my free hand, the one not covering my face.

"I stopped reading because I was thrilled. Crow liking you is a dream come true. It would sure keep her mind off my Basil, if you know what I mean. He sure seems to be preoccupied with her of late."

Mel quietly stood with Crow's notebook in hand, and walked it back to my cubicle, finishing the delivery and feeling good for the first time in weeks. She would let Crow sleep, seeing as she was the nocturnal type.

Then the quiet door opened again. Mel dropped down. The door closed gently.

"Right there I should have stood up, but it was so early, and I wasn't supposed to be there. That's when I heard kissing and Crow whispering, 'Shane.' Honestly, I started smiling. But when I peeked up, expecting to see you, it was, uh, it was Basil.

"Then what?" I whispered.

"What do you mean?" She stiffened. "Haven't you heard what I've been saying?"

"Believe me, I've heard. Then what?"

Mel shifted. "Basil yelled."

"Why?"

"Based on his eye, I think Crow hit him."

"Crow did hit him. Two fists to the face and a knee to the groin." I bowed my head.

Mel took a deep breath. "You don't know that. And even if she did, it doesn't change anything. Crow must have realized it was Basil and not you, at least for a little bit. She always knows what she's doing."

"She's been sleep deprived for ten years. She barely knew her own name, and she stopped Basil, who, by the way, has deteriorated from decent guy to something between scum and monster." I looked up at Mel. "Crow was pretty heroic, if you ask me."

"You think this is Basil's fault?" Mel bristled, the muscles in her face twitching and tightening. "What I saw this morning started long ago. Long before you showed up. There's a history here, a secret one. I know about their little darkroom rendezvous, their washroom grope sessions. She sets the traps. He happens to walk into them. He's been so confused—"

"Let me get this straight. I need to be sure I follow you. . . ." I leaned forward. "Crow is sleeping, clearly waiting for me. Basil touches her, and she whacks him in the eye. And you blame her? That's what we're talking about here?"

Mel's face darkened. "She's had a hold on him since elementary school, and day after day I put up with it. I put up with her half-dead looks that suck Basil in like a vacuum. I never fought back . . . but that ends now. I'm not losing Basil."

There was a long silence here, a gathering of thoughts, at least on my part.

"Maybe she just needed a friend, you know?"

"A friend," Mel scoffed. "Right."

I raised my eyebrows. "So what now?"

"Believe me, Shane. I don't know what she's told you, but she doesn't care about you or me or anybody except her precious sister. She would drop anything for her, and that fact is my only hope, because for Addy, she'd even drop my Basil."

The woozy feeling returned.

"So what if we had something to occupy her, just until her Basil fetish is dead once and for all?" She brightened. "And here's the best part: What if it helped you, too? Helped you get Crow back."

I stared at her blank-faced, not something you normally can sense about yourself. But I felt so numb, expression wasn't possible.

"I'm sure you know, Adele's seeing this loser from Hope Home. What you probably don't know is that, until the end of middle school, Crow protected Addy from her stepdad, a real sicko. She told Basil about it just last year. I guess she'd sit up all night, a little girl with a big knife."

And I had entrusted my secret to Basil, a little boy with a big mouth.

I held up my hand. I didn't need the replay.

"Well, that's over for her, but if Crow thought someone else was a threat to Addy, it would dominate her thoughts." She bit her lip. "Look, I'm not talking cruelty. The outcome would be best for everyone, including Crow."

My brain glazed over. I was witnessing the rumor hatch. The one that I had believed and lived to prevent, and that eventually took my life. A rumor started by a friend. The revelation was too much.

Mel continued, "The two of us will say, oh, this is perfect because you work with him, the two of us will say that the only reason Will is seeing Addy is to get her alone, which, knowing guys, no offense—"she chuckled—"is probably true, but that will be enough to set Crow's protective instincts on fire."

"Yeah, it would."

"She'll focus her time protecting Addy from Will."

"Yeah, she will."

Mel clapped hands together as if planning a birthday party. "Let's make it specific. We need a day, a target day for Will's move." She stared at me, and I dropped my gaze. "Let's push it into the future because that will keep her mind whirring for some time and give me a chance to work some sense back into Basil's brain." She drummed her fingernails on the piano bench. "Got it! Prom night. Will's sure to ask Addy. Let's say he's planning this for prom night. That's May 1. Sound good?"

"Mayday," I whispered.

"In the meantime, I get Basil back, and after the prom, after Crow busts up Will's plan, which is really *our* plan, and she's thinking normally again, you get her!"

No, I won't.

I stood and shook my head. "You don't know what you're doing. What you're setting in motion."

"This isn't what I asked for." Mel rose and paused. "Crow's a friend. There's just no other way." She opened the door and glanced over her shoulder. "Honest. Everyone will thank me when this is over."

Have you ever witnessed the beginning of the end? A point in time when the dots fell into place and only you could see the complete picture? The crash, my attempt to rid Will from Addy's life—it was all based on a lie.

I have no proof Will ever set out to hurt Adele.

CHAPTER 19

THE THOUGHTS OF C. RAINE

People can't concentrate properly on blowing other people to pieces if their minds are poisoned by thoughts suitable to the twenty-fifth of December.

Ogden Nash

AS MENTIONED, I DID NOT RETURN TO THE GUIDANCE OFFICE. That's not completely true. I ducked back in to find, as Mel reported, a notebook filled with all Crow knew of Will. On another day I would have been overjoyed. This day I did not care. This day I needed to find Crow.

I remembered where I went the first time around, after Basil had attempted to stake his claim.

The darkroom had been locked; of all the days for Mr. Gerald, the custodian, to get serious. I ran to the girls' lavatory, locked the stall, and shook. I stayed there the entire day, listening as Basil's bravado floated in on wings of female voice. With each version, the assault's account twisted, bringing me closer to the role of instigator and Basil nearer the position of victim. I must've heard the story twenty times—it pleased the school to hear of me as weak.

I remember feeling I deserved it, somehow. That although I remembered his attack from within a thick fog, I must have deserved it. So I listened and sat until Mel and Julie Richear walked in. Upon hearing Mel's voice, I relaxed and forced cramped legs to stand. But the topic of their conversation strayed from convention and kept me hidden where I was.

"That's what I heard him say," Mel's voice echoed loud.

I peeked at her through the crack in the stall, watched as she continued. "On prom night. He'll pick her up, take her to the hotel, and—"

"You're kidding, that's sick. Have you told Addy yet?"

"I haven't seen her. But I'll do one better. I'll tell Crow. She'll know what to do. She knows her sister better than anybody, so I'll let her take care of the pervert. There's no way she'll let Will touch Adele."

Julie slung back her hair. "I never thought I'd say it, but this is one time you want Crow as your sister. Hey, did I hear right that she and Basil . . ."

I opened the stall door and emerged into an empty bathroom. I stared at myself, useless piece of junk that I was. Right then I made a vow that would haunt me the rest of my brief life.

Will and his friends would not get near my sister.

It seemed the only way to salvage my existence.

⸺

I stood around the girls' bathroom waiting for Crow to come out, but a guy can stand near that entrance for only so long, and I made frequent trips through the halls to pass the time. When the final bell rang and the whoop went up for Christmas break, Crow still had not appeared.

Sadie was right; I was affecting events. Crow's life was accelerating. After all, the first time around, Basil attacked me in April. Maybe this day the darkroom door had been open. Maybe Crow spent her hours there and never overheard Mel's lie about Will. Given the season, maybe Mel found some Christmas cheer and thought better of spreading the rumor.

Maybe she never did spread poison about Addy and Will.

I strolled toward the bus and eased inside. I sat and Thomas scooted across the aisle, took a place beside me. "The school is buzzing today. Can't say I like what I heard."

"Whatever it was from whoever said it, don't believe it," I turned and grimaced. Will sat behind me, his head down. One look at his face, and I knew. The egg had hatched. The lie was alive. Though she did not care, Mel's words destroyed Will, too. Being a bad boy carried a certain mystique. Being a bad-boy pervert, not so much.

I reached back and tousled his hair. Don't know why, but it felt right, and he glanced up as if he didn't care. About anything.

"It's not true, Will." I cleared my throat. "What people are saying, I know it's not true."

"Tell me, Prophet, will Addy believe that?"

I shrugged. "Maybe she didn't hear."

He glanced away. I did, too.

⁓

"What's it like on Christmas Eve?" Mr. Loumans scooped a load of snow off the steps.

Hope Home was all decked out, and clearing the last bit of snow from the walk finished the job. "You know, up there." He poked heavenward with the handle of his shovel.

It's a big responsibility to paint a man's picture of the hereafter. Too big for me.

"Can't say. Sort of a trade secret."

I hoped that would suffice and pitched a shovelful off the bottom step. No go.

"Just a morsel." Loumans scraped at an ice chunk on the pavement. "A man lives a long time on this earth believing, hoping. Then, suddenly, a confirmation letter like you appears, but I'm not allowed to open it. Could you give me something to hang on to? To look forward to."

I thought a bit. "There's no tuna fish."

Mr. Loumans thought a moment, and set out laughing. "There you go. Ask a foolish question, and there you go."

Will stepped out of the front door, wriggling inside his rented suit. "You look good, Will. You've worked hard. You deserve this." Mr. Loumans stepped up and straightened his tie.

"Mrs. Amy helped me with that. I've never worn one before."

"No," Mr. Loumans answered. "It's a very adequate Windsor, don't you think? Mr. Shane will be your chaperone. Have him home by eleven."

"Home by eleven." I turned and repeated to Will, "By eleven."

"Okay, Prophet. Take me over."

I grabbed the keys to the Impala from Mr. Loumans's outstretched hand and walked with Will toward the garage. "Did you get her a present?" I asked.

"Yeah." He dug in his pocket. "What do you think?"

He held up a silver chain.

"Nice, but have you noticed she always accessorizes in gold?"

"What the hell does that mean?"

"Forget it. I think I can help."

Will jittered in the passenger seat, genuinely nervous. He

was a lot of things, perhaps a lot of really unpleasant things, but he wasn't Monster Number 2. How dumb I'd been.

We pulled into a Best Buy. "She likes James Taylor, and her *Greatest Hits* CD is scratched beyond listening."

Will frowned, disappeared into the store, and reappeared a few minutes later.

"Okay," he said. "Got it." He removed the plastic case from his suit coat pocket.

It was my turn to frown.

"You didn't pay for that, did you?"

"I spent what I had on the silver thing."

I rubbed my face. "Wait here." I walked inside to even up, and it dawned on me I had nothing for Crow. I swooped into the CD aisle. "dArKANgLe. Just the thing." I righted Will's wrong and paid at the cashier, rejoined Will in the car.

"Thanks," Will said. "I'll pay you back for all you've done."

Oh Lord, I hope not.

We pulled into Mom's buried driveway. Jude didn't believe in shoveling. Outside, one small, plastic Santa guarded the door. Jude had gone all out this year.

"Will, I'm supposed to have you home by eleven, but if you're a little late, don't sweat it." He grinned and opened his door, and I turned off the engine. Will poked his head back into the car. "You don't need to sit in the driveway."

"No, I, uh, need to sit inside. Crow invited me."

Will straightened, bent back down, then straightened again. "You and Crow?"

I shrugged. "No, I don't know why she invited me, really, there's no me and Crow."

"Oh, wow. Yesterday in school must've sucked for you, too."

"Pretty much."

I waited for the explosion, the kicking of the Impala, an act that said, Stay out of my life—but none came. Instead, Will smiled.

"Well then, Prophet, let's go inside." A hint of relief tinged his voice. "Honest, this is probably good. I'm a little nervous."

I glanced at the door and joined him and Santa.

You should be.

I let my head thud against the brick wall.

Three times Will rang the doorbell. Three times he frowned at me. "Aren't they here?"

"Yeah." I pointed. "They're all in there. Jude is sitting right by the door."

"Why doesn't he answer?"

"You're being 'seasoned.' It's one of his psychological tricks to gain the upper hand before he puts you through the Inquisition."

"I don't know what that mean—."

"Jude, the Monster, will ask you a series of questions, as if he has some authority over Addy, as if he's some overprotective dad instead of what he is, a freakish—" I raised my hand and zipped my lips.

Too much info. Sorry, Sadie.

Will tugged on his tie. "That's what he did to you on account of Crow?"

"No." I rubbed my face. "I could be an ax murderer, and it wouldn't matter. Crow's not Addy."

The door swung open, and Jude appeared. My face tightened, and then eased. I didn't want him dead, and the realization shocked me. He looked like a different monster. Shorter, older, weaker. He seemed sick and pale, more in need of a hospital than a morgue.

"Come in, boys."

We stepped into the entryway.

"Crap!" Will turned his head this way and that. His Freudian was right on the money.

We moved forward single file through a thin, cleared space in the entryway. Jude *had* shoveled for Christmas Eve.

An explanation is in order: one that reaches clear back to when I was thirteen, to the day after Addy's horror. When Mom came back from her retreat that next morning, she found the two of us locked in the bathroom. Addy led her into our room, where Mom stared at the dresser and the broken glass and the ripped clothing. I think she came to the same conclusion I had: evil had come.

And something inside her snapped.

"Whatever happened will never happen again."

This was all she said.

Whatever happened? I told her what had happened— loudly, clearly.

She yelled her line back into my face. It was her wall. The only way, I believe, she could continue living with herself. After all, self-blame takes a strong constitution. Courage, really, to say, Yeah, I shouldn't have done it. I shouldn't have gone.

But I didn't let up. I shouted and shouted until she brought out the one weapon that could silence me.

"It would never have happened if your father were here!"

And the guilt I felt about Jude's attack joined hands with the guilt I felt about Dad, and the weight of the two overwhelmed. I went into the tree house and sobbed.

But deep inside, Mom must've known that she factored into the mix, too. She had ceded control to Jude, and she determined never to do so again. That night, I listened to her raised voice, and her altered declaration:

"If this happens again, you will be playing doctor behind bars, with people your own size."

The next morning we noticed two changes. The first, Jude had disappeared, presumably to speak at a therapist convention. As conventions rarely are monthlong events, it didn't take long to piece together the truth: Jude's continued presence in Mom's home depended on his undergoing intense in-patient therapy. It was about time that Jude became a victim of his own psycho-babble.

The second discernable change was more comforting than the first, though it would cost Mom her life.

She did not leave for work.

Nor did she the following day, or the following week. She wandered around the house, whispering her mantra.

"Whatever happened will never happen again."

In the years that followed, Mom rarely left the home. She could not restore what had been taken, and though Jude was not indicted, Mom could see to it that a sentence was served. Her conscience would force her to serve it. She became the house's vigilant eyes and ears, a responsibility I slowly relinquished.

Jude called it agoraphobia. Apparently, he felt it an acceptable malady, much like, say, pedophilia.

I felt for my mother. I knew her strange kind of hell: a fear that stole sleep and haunted dreams, a fear demanding ultimate sacrifice. Little things like keeping house and keeping herself up no longer mattered.

Yes, it was the season of giving, but for Mom and Dad, Addy and me, there was nothing left to give; Jude had already taken it all.

Merry Christmas.

CHAPTER 20

THE THOUGHTS OF C. RAINE

There are two things that are more difficult than making an after-dinner speech: climbing a wall which is leaning toward you and kissing a girl who is leaning away from you.

Winston Churchill

JUDE SIZED UP BOTH OF US WITHOUT A HANDSHAKE. "Which of you is Will?"

Will was busy staring around the entryway. "What is all this crap? It's worse than the dump."

"We haven't gotten around to house cleaning, and I assume that comment correctly tags you as Will. Follow me." Jude worked his way into the living room. Will followed, toppling stacks of magazines as he went.

They sat down on opposing chairs, and I rolled my eyes. This would take a while. I plunked down in the entryway, settled back against the closet, and sighed. The place *was* a pit. It took Will's mouth and Shane's eyes for me to realize it.

For a minute, Jude said nothing. Will's leg bounced, and

the Monster picked at his fingernails. He would draw this out as long as he could.

"Why should I let you see my precious Adele?"

If he was a dad, a normal dad, that sentence might sit fine, but not after. What is it about being male that authorizes you to claim people?

"She's great." Will shrugged. "She invited me over. I wasn't planning on proposing." He chuckled, looked at me and then back to Jude, and his chuckle vanished.

Jude licked his lips. "What *were* you planning on doing?"

Will peeked at me, and his face twitched. I wagged my head. Jude's questions were a virus. *Let them run their course.*

"Oh, I thought I'd wait until you weren't looking, sneak her out, take her behind the house, and—"

"Do you have a car, Will?" Jude hissed.

"I used to."

"Right. What type of vehicle was it?"

Will's face shaded wistful. "Camaro, yellow. She was a beauty—not saying she was mine, but that's another story."

"Sure," said Jude. "If you were still in possession of said vehicle, and I, a stranger, came to your door and asked for the keys, would you give them to me?"

"Would money be accompanying the keys?"

"No."

"Then no."

Wrong answer.

"What if I promised to take good care of it?" Jude's lips curled, and he closed in for the kill. "I mean, I'd only be gone a few hours."

"Nobody takes my wheels."

Really wrong answer.

Jude wagged his pointer at Will. "But here you are, a stranger, asking to see my daughter, who is much more valuable than a car."

Game over.

Will scooted forward in his chair. "I didn't ask you for nothin'. I'm not takin' her nowhere. You seem like the kind of guy who wants to hold my hand and make sure I behave. Is that what you want to do, Mr. Jude? I suppose that could be arranged."

I loved that kid. I know I spent considerable soul time trying to end his life, but I loved him—his hard edge and soft center. In the face of Jude's insanity, Will held his ground and fought for Addy. Just like Crow. No wonder I judged him so quickly the first time around. He reminded me too much of myself.

Jude stood up, his psychology lying in pieces on the floor, and finally noticed me. "Crow's in her room. Good luck getting her out."

I started to walk and stopped. "This way?"

JONATHAN FRIESEN

"Through the kitchen and to your right, end of the hall."

"Hi, Adele." I quietly closed the bedroom door behind me. Addy stared up from her perch atop Crow's bed, her arm around her big sister. Crow gazed down, her focus on the book she treasured above all others.

In truth, it wasn't a book. It was a journal, filled with Dad's favorite philosophical quotations. Since high school, he'd kept a record of the quotes that impacted him, the ones that he was working through, those that were worthy of his attention. Divided into chapters, one for each year, the journal left a bread crumb trail of my dad's changing beliefs over time.

The Thoughts of C. Raine.

How many hours I'd spent poring over those pages.

It, and my locket, were my only record of the invisible man, the only tangible proof that the hole in my heart had at one point been filled.

I stood there, watching Crow, and it suddenly became clear. She wasn't reading. She was searching, searching for a dimly lit road that could weave through her darkness, her wasted life.

In her moments of personal agony, Crow always turned to Dad's thoughts, Dad's journal.

Crow always searched for her father.

My father.

I slumped back against the door. I was wrong about Will, and in order to avert the catastrophe of Mayday, Crow must also see it. This was still my quest, but my heart burned with a new flame. If my walkabout didn't end at my father's side—I fingered the locket—I would forever be searching.

"You must be Shane." Addy squeezed Crow. "He's here," she whispered, as if Crow wasn't, which was near the truth. Crow didn't flinch.

Addy exhaled hard. "Will?"

"He's being interrogated by Jude."

Her face lit up, and Crow's hardened. She flicked a glance at the door, then went back to her oak-floor gaze—but she was no longer alone. Hate kept her company. That much was clear from her face.

"How's he doing out there?" Addy asked.

"Remarkably well."

"Still, I'm going to go rescue him." Addy jumped up and paused. "Unless you need me, Crow. I'll stay."

Crow gave a tight shake of the head, and Addy bounded out, slamming the door behind her. I looked around at the room I knew so well, at the nice replacement window. It and the bathroom window were the only decent ones in the entire house.

My gaze fell on the scar that traced up Crow's forearm, a remnant of the fight with Jasmine and my first intervention in my life. I dropped to the floor and scooted away from the door. Didn't want her to feel trapped.

"Why did you come?" she asked, her gaze not leaving the journal.

"I, uh, I'm sorry. Was my invite rescinded?"

"You weren't in school yesterday."

"I was. I searched for you," I said. "You can be hard to find."

"Then you heard that I was busy with Basil, so why don't you get out of my house?"

"Because I'm not after whatever Basil got."

Crow thought for a second, tongued the inside of her cheek, and nodded. "Don't blame you."

"No." I scooted forward. "That's not what I meant. You're beautiful. If you knew how hard it was for me in the tree house . . .I'm just saying that's not why I came. I still want to be with you." I raised my hands and let them fall to my lap. "It's hard to explain."

Crow shot up her hand, and I froze.

"Basil and I, we've never. We didn't. I should say, he didn't. As soon as I figured out what was happening, I smacked him, and if I had had my knife—" She paused. "If you so much as touch any part of me during any point of this evening, Christmas Eve or not, I will kill you."

"I know."

She straightened, set the journal on the bed, and threw back her hair. She was drop-dead gorgeous. It wasn't a line.

"Okay then," she whispered. "You can stay. But don't be expecting an invitation to New Year's Eve. We'll just ride this one out."

"Fair." I stood and opened the door for her. She rose, shuffled forward, halted in the doorway. "Did you see Will?"

"Of course. I work with the kid. I brought him over."

"Guess I can't hold that against you." She sauntered out of the room.

⌣

Do you celebrate Christmas? If so, happy thoughts likely consume the affair. Smiling people, lying people. "Oh, that's what I always wanted." Hugs and thank-yous and wrapping paper flying through the air.

Maybe there's a crackling fire on a cold night with Bing Crosby crooning in the background. I imagine jolly isn't hard to find in such a place.

Consider this scene: a browning Christmas tree, no stand, propped up by piles of phone books and leaning against the basement wall. No decorations. No music. No food.

Add to the mirth six sardined people, none of whom want to be there, and six unwrapped gifts, thrown beneath the tree.

Perhaps, you might think, the Christmas spirit will infuse the night with joy.

"Here." That's Jude handing his wife a new toaster.

"Thank you." There's tight-lipped Mom. That toaster will join her other one. Therapists make good money, but after Jude discovered Goodwill, he felt no need to spend any on Mom.

Mom reached down and handed Jude a tie. No surprise there. She always gave Jude a tie. She admitted to me that they came from the Dollar Store, a fact that brought me immense pleasure.

This year, however, I almost snatched the tie from his hands.

It was Dad's tie. Strange what people cling to after relationships end. Lockets. Ties. This paisley beauty hid, untouched, in the back of the linen closet. Every time I went for a towel, I stared at it, crumpled, out of place, but a remnant of Dad nonetheless.

There Jude was, holding the sacred. Maybe Mom couldn't find anyone to shop for her this year, but no excuse gave her the right.

My anger didn't make sense; it was a cheap tie worn sparingly by a man who lived only in my memory. But inside I ached, and I wished Dad was beside me. At least I'd hear some Christmas carols and we'd have a tree stand.

"That looks like an old tie." I hissed. "Where'd you get it?"

Crow stared at me. I didn't look back.

Jude raised it high in a triumphant display of the gift.

"This transfer, this exchange, is a family matter, Shane. It's a family secret."

"No, Jude," Crow said quietly. "That's my dad's tie."

Jude cleared his throat. "You and Shane are under no compulsion to stay. You and your friend may go crawl beneath the rock you live under."

So can you.

"Oh, wow, is that for me?" Adele broke in, reached beneath the tree, and retrieved her Macy's gift certificate. She then handed Crow her present, a gift card for the Book Emporium.

Will watched me the whole time, his twitchy hands eager to produce his present. The longer I gazed at him, the more certain I became: he was not in the same room. Nor was he in the same moment, or with the same people.

His face was filled with regret.

He was captive to a memory.

Finally, I gave the nod, and he shook free from his prison.

"I have something!" Words exploded from his lips, and Mom forced a smile.

"Well, Will. We are waiting with bated breath." Jude offered his most satisfied smile and folded his hands. "It's good to see that at least one youth remembers the honored tradition of gifting the parents."

"Sorry. Never heard of that tradition. We, uh, had our own." Will turned the CD over in his hands. "Dad and me, well, it was our job to chop down the tree. Just the two of us, wandering among hundreds of them at the tree farm. They were either too tall or too short or too thin near the base and finally . . . finally, he'd say, 'You go pick, son. I trust you to bring me the best. Nothing but perfection will do.'" Will glanced at our dead pine. "Damn hard to be perfect, you know?" he whispered, slapping the CD a few times. "Damn hard." He slowly turned and handed his gift to Adele.

"Merry Christmas."

She stared down at it, expressionless. Will, too, seemed lost in thought, and a strange heaviness descended in the room.

Pop! Adele broke free from her state and leaped onto Will's lap and hugged him something special. "How did you know? How could you have known?"

Will shrugged and glanced around, keeping his hands high in the air. A good move, based on Jude's and Crow's scowls. He glanced around the room, and his gaze landed on me. "I, uh, there's something I need to do. Say, Addy"—his stare never left me—"you want to go on a walk?"

Adele furrowed her brow. "Yeah, I'll come. Are you all right?"

"I think I am," Will said, breaking into a broad smile. "I think I finally am."

Adele stood, pulled Will to his feet. "Well, this really has been special. She leaned over and gave Crow a hug, while Will walked over to me. "Thanks, Prophet," he whispered. "For everything. Tell Mr. L that, well, just tell him."

Suddenly, I knew. Will was heading out on a walkabout of his own that would, indeed, end beside his father. And Addy? He was taking her away in the process.

I burned, not with anger or fear, but envy.

———

The two hurried upstairs, where the front door opened and shut.

"Ahem. Crow, here you go." I grinned. "Hope you like it."

I tossed her CD across the room; she caught it, examined it, looked at me, and nodded. I knew it was the best she could do.

Nobody spoke for minutes. Crow's leg bounced, and her mind whirred. Suddenly, she gasped, "That little snake!"

I cleared my throat. "I think Crow and I will go for a walk, too."

We rose, climbed the stairs, and Crow dashed into her room, came out wild-eyed. "Her bag's gone."

"Yeah, I gathered that downstairs."

Crow bit her lip. "He's not going to get away with it. He's a Monster, and he's not going to get away with it. She doesn't know. I don't know why I didn't tell her but I didn't, and so she doesn't know and now look at them."

"Addy likely heard the same thing you heard. It doesn't seem to worry her."

"My sister doesn't understand."

Crow ran back into her room and dashed out with a backpack. "I need to go." She kicked a pile aside, yanked open the closet door, and grabbed her black leather jacket. "See ya, Shane."

I reached for her arm, then recoiled. "Let me come."

"You don't get what's happening here. There's no way you could. I'm not getting eggnog. I'm not coming back. Not until I find them. Go back to your nice life."

I turned my back and slowly slipped my hand into my pocket.

I flipped open the locket and peeked down. A reddish glow, eerie, unnatural.

There was so little time.

"Let me come," I said quietly.

"You don't quit." Crow faced me square, waiting, I think, for me to change my mind.

"Okay, Shane Owen." She peeked out the front window. "Can we take the car?"

"Maybe. It's not mine. But that reminds me, I do need something from my cottage."

The something was, of course, Crow's notebook on Will. We drove the car back to Hope Home, and the two of us ran up the walk. Mr. Loumans met us in the doorway and shushed the wolf whistles from Eddie and Sean.

"What's wrong?" he asked.

I lowered my voice. "Will took off. It was expected."

Mr. Loumans breathed deeply, as if he'd considered this a plausible outcome of the evening. "What now?"

"I go after him."

Mr. Loumans thought a moment. "Sure you do. And where does this young lady fit into the sequence?"

"Will left with my sister," Crow spurted.

Mr. Loumans stepped out into the cold and folded his arms. "For such a night as this, were you not sent?" He shook his head and clasped his hands. "To be a part of such divine interventions must be a thrilling experience. May I ask, is she also—"

"Much more immortal than she's letting on," I said.

"Ah. Well, I will trust you know what is best. Keep me abreast of your affairs." His face grew haggard. "You know, of all the boys, Will has a special place in my heart. He has no place to go. Care for him."

"I will, sir." I turned to Crow. "Wait here." I dashed into my cottage and scooped up the notebook. When I returned to Hope Home's front door, I found two statues. Neither Crow nor Mr. Loumans appeared to have moved.

I broke the weighty silence. "I do have one request. Odds are they're heading to the train depot. May we take the Impala and leave it there?"

"Would a man hold back his donkey from the Good Lord? Should I hold back my transport from his workers?"

"Thanks." I peeked at Crow, who stared in horror at Mr. Loumans. Understanding had clearly taken hold. "I'll call you soon with word."

―

We turned and dashed toward the idling car. Inside with Crow, I fishtailed out of the driveway.

Crow rubbed her hands up and down her thighs. "Did I follow that correctly? Does the man who owns this car think you're an angel?"

"He does."

"And now he believes I'm one, too?" She stuffed the notebook in her pack.

"Possible."

There was a long silence. "Are you?" Crow asked.

This question, it dawned on me, could solve my dilemma. Perhaps straight from a spirit who stands in the presence of the living God, Crow might accept that the rumor that fueled her anger and this search was bogus. But I was discovering that Shane had reached his quota of mistruths. I could not speak another.

"No, I'm not."

Crow was no fool. She cast me a sideways glance. "'Cause it would sure explain a lot."

"Yeah, it would."

Silently, we sped through the night.

CHAPTER 21

THE THOUGHTS OF C. RAINE

With the catching ends the pleasure of the chase.
Abraham Lincoln

WE WANDERED THE VACANT DEPOT ON CHRISTMAS EVE. It looked every bit the train cemetery.

"Do trains run on Christmas?" I asked, and pounded the side of a rail car.

Crow shook her head. "Don't know. I really don't know. But she's smart. She wouldn't hitchhike. And there's no bus service to where we're going. . . . I taught her to hop a train."

I turned a complete circle, watching the wind whisk away my breath. I leaned against a nearby boxcar. "Maybe we should let 'em go. They won't stay gone forever."

Crow's gaze burned into me. "You have no idea what's at stake for her, or what Addy's been through, or what your little beast has planned."

"'My little beast'? Interesting." I looked off, and then

back at her. "And you know his intentions? For certain."

She nodded.

"Reliable source, then?"

She opened and closed her mouth. "A twisted one, I'll give you that, but the source didn't know I was listening."

"And you find the girls' bathroom to be a good place to gather information, in general?"

Crow stuck her finger in my chest. "I never told you where I first heard it."

I raised both my hands. "I was standing outside of the bathroom when Mel and a friend walked out. They talked about it all the way down the hall. I couldn't find you all day long. Where else would you be hiding out?" I peeked down at her finger. "And for the record, my chest did not initiate this contact."

Crow pulled back. "You drive a person crazy."

The train on which I leaned lurched forward, and I stumbled to the ground, my leg slipping onto the track. "Whoa." I yanked it back. "Almost one-legged Shane. I don't think Sadie could fix that."

"There." Crow pointed into the darkness. Twenty cars up, a silhouetted arm reached out of a boxcar, stretching toward a suit walking alongside the slow-moving train.

Crow cursed. "That would be Will. I hope *he* falls beneath the tracks."

"So harsh, Crow." I paused and brushed snow off my jeans.

"What now, you want me to yell and scream?"

"No, he'll jump in, we'll miss our chance, and it'll be too late. For now, we follow." She flung her pack into a boxcar and jogged alongside the quickening train. I took off after. We sped to a sprint, lined up with the car's mouth, and leaped. I landed with a thud. Crow landed on top of me.

"Just for the record—"

"Shut up, Shane." She pushed off me, and in the darkness, I caught a tight grin. Progress.

—

North. There are many good times to go north in Minnesota, many good reasons if hunting or ice fishing is your thing.

But they weren't mine, and with the temperature dropping below zero and the wind rushing in, I felt quite certain that Shane, my shell, was not a cold-weather type of guy. He was probably from New Mexico or Florida or someplace where old folk flee to when their hardy Minnesota years have passed.

I shivered in the corner and marveled at Crow, whose image I will never forget.

She sat cross-legged in the open boxcar mouth, her black leather jacket and jeans providing little more than a windbreak. She neither shivered nor slept. She stared into the night, black hair streaming in the freezing breeze, whipping across her face. Of all the situations in which I saw her, in none was she so alluring as in that pose.

Alluring, but untouchable. Though I sure longed for some body heat.

"You, uh, familiar with expeditions to the Antarctic?" I asked. She did not flinch. "Right. Colonel Jenks and his hand-picked crew headed out, a little too close to winter. The water froze around them. They radioed for help, but the signal never reached a soul."

"So they ate each other or something," Crow said. "Are you hungry or what?"

"No, they didn't, well, yes, a few did eat each other, but that's not the issue here."

"You're cold."

"Well, the men, the ones who did not eat each other, huddled in very platonic fashion, and the warmth—"

"Kept them alive."

"Actually, no, they all died, but I bet they stayed a little warmer toward the end there."

Crow spun around. "You wanted to come!"

"That has nothing to do with the fact that I'm about to lose certain body parts."

"I might consider your request if you did."

I had no response to that.

I hunkered down in the corner, my mind drifting into frost-induced sleep. In the frigid morning, I awoke from this dream:

Crow scooted over to where I huddled, unbuttoned

my thin flannel jacket, and crawled inside, drawing it back around us. She laid her black leather on top, pressed her face into my chest, and cried. Soft, warm tears soaked through my sweatshirt. Her arms wrapped around me, and mine wrapped around her, and we held each other, our bodies bobbing with the roll of the boxcar.

I opened my eyes to find my jacket buttoned and Crow back on her perch. But I felt warm through and through, except for my chest.

My sweatshirt was damp.

The train rumbled on, and I stretched and shuffled next to Crow, swung my legs over the edge.

"Where do you think we're going?"

She reached into her backpack, grabbed the notebook, and slapped it against my chest. "Page three."

I opened it and read aloud. **Will Kroft, 17 years old. Born in Morneau, Minnesota. His father still pastors a small Baptist church outside of town. Mother flew the coop when he was a kid.**

"Will's a pastor's kid?" I slapped shut the pages.

"Yeah, and I'm an angel." Crow rolled her eyes. "But it's what he told Addy."

"So you think they're heading to Morneau?"

She tapped the notebook on my lap. "You should read it. There might be things in there even you don't know. He's a weasel. The letter he wrote to Addy at the end is rather brilliant. I copied it word for word while she slept."

The train rumbled through Cambridge and Grandy. I slowly flipped through the notebook. The front of each page held handwritten accounts of Adele and Will's interactions; Crow had scrawled her interpretations on the flip side.

"You write well, Crow."

"I know. Read his letter."

I paged to the end, scanned the note, and scooted back.

> Dear Adele,
> Do you remember your dad? The sound
> of his footsteps heavy on the stairs or the
> smell of him, a scent which, when it finally
> disappeared, felt a little like a second death?

I did remember my dad's footsteps—my real dad's—his safe footsteps outside our door.

> You were young when you lost your dad.
> That's no less horrible, but perhaps less
> costly. Except in your case.

> Three years ago today, I began a slow
> walk south from Morneau, south from the
> reverend. While he was pointing folks to
> heaven, I was giving him hell, so I figured

it was a decent decision, one both he and I would agree to . . . that is, if we spoke.

Three years have gone by, and it may well be going great for him. But it's not for me. I was fortunate. Mr. L found me downtown, and if a kid needs a substitute dad, you could not ask for better. But I can't take it anymore. The moralizing, the lessons. It's not that I can't stand Mr. L, it's that he reminds of what I lost, what I left.

Time has erased most of the anger, and all the other reasons I left in the first place, though I know those reasons are still likely there. But I want to go home.

So I'm asking you to think about coming with me. I'll understand if you say no, though quite honestly, other than Crow, I don't know what would tether you here.

I do know that I want you to come with me. Think about it, Adele.

Will.

I set down the pad. "He wrote this? He doesn't know half these words. Who did he pay?"

"Snake," Crow whispered. "Addy could not turn that down. Not innocent Addy. The thing's poetic."

And accurate. Mr. Loumans had the same effect on me. He reminded me of what I'd lost, planted in me the desire to find the one man I could never leave, though he may have left me.

Cameron Raine. What would I ask him if I saw him again? Would he recognize my face? Well, Crow's face.

"It's a good letter," I whispered.

"See how he set it all up?" Crow began to rock. "The poor, abused reverend's son, forced out of his hometown and lost in the big city. Suddenly stricken by conscience and going back to make things right. That's not good, that's genius."

I waited a few seconds. "Suppose there's always a chance the kid's all right, and the letter's true."

Crow looked over sharply. "If it is true, I will die."

Later, I thought over her statement, so forcefully predicted. As I rewound the tape of all her words, turns out this was her only prophecy.

Scary.

The train rumbled into Morneau, and Crow peeked out of the car.

"They're getting off. He has her now. Will knows this

place. He probably called his old friends. We're Addy's only hope." Crow slapped my shoulder. "They've left the depot."

She grabbed her bag, I held the notebook tight, and we jumped onto the platform. Crow yanked me inside the vacant depot. In the distance, two figures tramped away from us onto a snow-packed road.

"Keep an eye on them." She grabbed her smartphone from her coat pocket. "Morneau. Population two thousand. They're heading away from town."

"Any churches that way?" I asked.

Crow dropped her arms. "Let the letter go. It's lies. I need *you* to follow them." She flattened down her black leather. "We're in Hicksville. I'm too visible here. You have your phone, right?"

I patted my flannel and rubbed the pocket. Lying was easier if I didn't actually speak.

"I'm going into town to find out what I can about Will. I'll need more than bathroom stories to convince Addy's she's in danger."

I frowned, and so did Crow. "You wanted to be useful, so here's your chance. Don't let Will touch her, and if he does—"

"What?" I asked. "What do you want me to do?"

I pushed out the door and hauled myself onto the snow-packed road, stopped, and called back. "I've never been wrong yet, and I believe every word of that letter."

Crow whipped around and stormed off toward the grain elevator and the water tower and what looked to be downtown Morneau.

The end of my junior year, on what had become the only trendy day to go to school, the administration packed up every student, all two thousand of us, and shipped us off to Valleyfair Amusement Park, the closest thing Minnesota has to Six Flags.

Did I tell you that Adele adored me? Idolized me? It's true, but on days like this, I'm not the one she wanted to hang with. She had other friends—Jacque Basset and Lori Hammond, to be exact—friends who would drop their lives for her. If you knew Addy, you knew why. Adele was not only beautiful and smart and witty, she was quick with a laugh and long to listen. I realize perfect is an overused adjective, but every so often, you meet a perfect person. Normally, they nauseate. But Adele was so perfect you couldn't even hate her. She treated you better than herself.

That's sick.

Back to Valleyfair.

It possessed typical amusement-park fare: killer rides, greasy food, an impressive water park . . . and hounds. Hounds ran in packs of threes or fours. They entered through the turnstiles and quickly ditched their shirts in order to place their few chest hairs on display. Actually, only two of them posed. The others were skinny and knew it.

Here, my stint in Shane provided insight. The leader, normally the loud, chiseled one, jostled with the number two in command. The others tagged along with tongues wagging, satisfied to be in the presence of such beefy hounds. These others mutts laughed and joked as if they belonged, but inside they felt like crap.

Unsupervised hook-up venues like Valleyfair drew hounds like vomit, and I took it on myself to watch Adele from a distance. With crowds thick, it was a chore to keep a visual, but over the years, I'd honed my Adele-o-meter. At first, a few of my disciples accompanied me, eager to convince me they gave a rip, but soon they drifted, leaving me alone to keep up the vigil.

Many mangy packs approached Adele on my junior-year trip, but the last group, the group of three? They were different.

Shirtless and his two followers mastered the art of sniffing and hunting. I placed myself behind the concession booth not ten feet from Adele and marveled. This lead hound was good.

He first addressed Jacque and Lori, and set them to giggling.

"Smart hound," I whispered. All hounds needed to get by the friends. They formed the moat around the castle. Too bad that in Adele's case, the moat was pretty shallow. Shirtless quickly turned his attention to the prize. He got Addy talking, not a good thing, and then cast his line.

"We're heading over to the water park. Why don't you come?"

Adele had been to the water park. The hound could see that, no doubt enjoying the sight of her wet. And this is where I wished Addy'd spent a little more time with Nietzsche, for how true it is that "the man of knowledge must be able not only to love his enemies but also to hate his friends."

"Come on, Adele." Jacque whined like a child. As if she believed, even for a second, that this invitation had anything to do with her. I saw Adele wavering. Time to spring.

"Hey, Adele!" I quickly approached.

She turned and gave me a big hug. "Hey, Crow. Are you alone? Because we were thinking of heading to the water park. Want to come?"

I don't know who looked more disappointed, Shirtless or Addy's friends. I looked down at my black on black outfit. "I didn't dress for it, but yeah, it's nice of you to invite me."

"Like you ever dress for it!" Adele smiled. "Guys, this is my sister, Crow. Crow, I forgot their names."

I stepped toward them and whispered, "Shirtless dog."

I backhanded the leader's chest. "And these are your two puppies. Cute little family you have here."

"You freak." Shirtless frowned and backhanded the shocked dog standing beside him. "Let's go."

"Freak? You're calling my sister a freak? Yeah, just keep on walking. I'm sorry, Crow, you don't deserve that. Hang with us the rest of today." She hugged my arm.

—

I thought of Shirtless as I marched, lost and alone, a solitary figure surrounded by pine trees green and white. I should have let Addy go to the water park. The hound might have been a pretty decent guy.

CHAPTER 22

THE THOUGHTS OF C. RAINE

Every mile is two in winter.
George Herbert

THE WIND PICKED UP. All warmth from my boxcar dream had
faded, and my tennis shoes provided precious little by way
of frost protection. I'd gone on long winter walks before,
mainly two-hour hikes between the Shack and Mom's
house, and mainly with Basil. But that route had rest
stops along the way, namely Perkins and Duke's All-Night
Coffee.

There was no Perkins on this road.

Just miles of farmland, stretching out as far as I could
see. Spaces widened the farther I wandered from Morneau,
and fewer trees lined the road, unfortunate as the occasional
shelterbelt provided a brief break from the wind. I tugged the
flannel around me, peeked at the sky, and stopped.

Never one to pay too much attention to the weather, I, when Crow, always stared down as I loped. It was easier to keep track of my steps. This was not so with Shane, which is why I actually saw it happen; I witnessed a clear blue sky turn cloudy.

Not a big deal, you might think. You've seen clouds roll in, too, but I wager you haven't seen a line of thick gray rise on the horizon and advance toward you—with speed. A perfect line, like a gray sheet pulled over a bed of blue. The front seam of that sheet reached a point directly overhead, and I stared up at a sky *exactly* one half blue and one half gray. Have you ever seen that?

Didn't think so.

Neither Will nor Adele showed any concern, at least from the rear and from a distance. No staring, no finger-pointing, no screams, "It's the end of the world!"

"Where you going, Shane?"

I slowly lowered my gaze and turned. "Hi, Sadie."

My syrupy visitor walked on by, knitting the whole way, something akin to driving and texting, albeit on a smaller scale. "Oh, honey. You're at it again. I warned you about shaping others' futures. The first time around, Will and Addy didn't come out here until just before Mayday, and here we are at Christmas."

"Wait!" I jogged up to her. "I've really cut down. I've held my tongue. There's so much more I could have said."

"I know, child. That's not why I'm here." She handed me a sweater. "Try this. Should just about fit." I whipped off my flannel and squeezed into the warmest sweater I'd felt. I wriggled back into my coat.

"Thank you. I was dying out here."

"An interesting turn of phrase coming from you, but point taken." She grinned quickly, her face returning to solemn. "You ain't had much time to look at that locket."

"Was I supposed to?" I dug in my jeans. Again, the locket felt heavy in my hand and I flipped it open.

Dark red. Drippy red.

My heartbeat quickened. "What's happening?"

"Coraline, I mean Lifeless, is fixing to wake. I don't know the moments you have left here, but it's about to fade to black. She's clinging precarious to shallow sleep."

I knew all about shallow sleep, and my shoulders weakened. "My time's going to run out before Mayday, isn't it?"

Sadie paused in her knitting.

We wandered in silence. I do not remember how long.

"I failed again," I whispered. "Two chances and every advantage, and I failed again." I gritted my teeth and stopped, stared up at the two-tone sky. "You may as well take me now."

From the corner of my eye, I saw Sadie reach out her hand. I closed my eyes and stretched trembling fingers out toward her.

Sadie slapped a pair of wool socks into my palm. "So impulsive."

I frowned, balanced against a fence post, and slipped off frozen shoes.

"Be careful now, that be electric fencing. Shane's tough, but that'd push it."

I straightened and finished the job. "I won't be around to help Addy. What's left for me here?"

"Your first good question." Sadie drew a deep breath. "I think even you'd admit you done a fair piece of work. You aren't the same you I spoke to at the beginning of your walkabout. You're gentler."

"Being a wuss does little good."

"And you believe some different things about people. About Thomas and Will and Basil. You see things clearer."

"But if I can't make Crow see it—"

"And maybe most of all there's an itching inside, something that, if I were to leave you here until Lifeless wakes, you might be able to attend to. If you get a move on."

"An itching? I do think about Crow a lot, well, Crow and . . ."

Dad.

"Your father, Coraline. Your father be alive. He's not far." She pointed to my pocket. "There's a reason I gave you the locket. The one from him. I told you not to worry about Adele.

I told you not to spend this time trying to cheat death. This time was always for you, you and your dad. Haven't you felt it, Coraline? Bits and pieces of what was, what could have been, what should have been between the two of you? And here you done gobbled up sacred time trying to save someone who needs no saving."

I feel it.

"I tell you this now because I could not before. We supposed to leave you to your own discoveries, your own conclusions during your walkabout, but time is short. Hear this: Your father didn't do right by you. He didn't stay for you, fight for you. He lay on your shoulders more than they was meant to bear." She peeked up, and lowered her voice. "But imperfect as the man is, he never stopped loving you."

Sadie was gone. Where she stood lay another pair of mittens. "Thanks, Sadie."

I picked them up, stuffed in my hands, and felt a crinkle. I pulled out a piece of paper and read the address.

"No way."

I slipped the scrap into my back pocket and retrieved Dad's locket once more. The red blazed under the brilliant sun. All its former colors—green, yellow, and red—I knew from Lifeless's dream. I knew what they meant. Green was life; the family was happy, Dad was there. Yellow was a warning of Jude the Destroyer. Red was pain and the end of all things.

But that's where the dream colors stopped . . .and my philosophy started.

I didn't know what happened after the end.

I didn't know black, the color I wore in life, the color that followed death.

I glanced up, and the clouds were gone.

Time. I need to get back. I need to get back with Crow. She needs to know.

I looked ahead and squinted.

Will and Adele were gone, too.

CHAPTER 23

THE THOUGHTS OF C. RAINE

Diogenes struck the father when the son swore.
Robert Burton, "Anatomy of Melancholy,"
Democritus to the Reader, 1621

I'D NEVER BEEN A TRACKER. Paw prints from tree to tree meant squirrel, but that was the extent of my ability. The hardpack left only an occasional tread imprint of Will's dress shoe when it strayed and caught fresh powder at the road's edge. But when I reached two distinct sets of tracks leading off into a field, it almost had to be them, and I set my face against the wind.

I followed them into the woods. There was only the crunch of the snow and the amplified sound of breath, and I felt small and inconsequential. But the spaces of winter left room for thoughts of Dad, and I wished I could recall taking even one walk together.

The trees thinned out, and I emerged onto a smaller road. There, the two tracks merged, and separated, one heading left and the other right.

"Great."

I chose the smaller print and quickened my step, rounding a curve in time to see a church in the middle of nowhere, a tiny house at its side, and Adele slipping in between them.

Pulling my flannel up around my face, I jogged nearer, passed the house, and rounded the church, where I paused at the sign out front.

HILLTOP BAPTIST

PASTOR WILL KROFT SR.

ALL WELCOME!

"Huh. He did tell the truth," I muttered. "That sneaky kid."

I walked beyond the church's glass door, circled the entire building, and approached the entrance to the house. I breathed deep and knocked.

There was a pause, and the door flew open. Adele rushed into my arms, pushed back out, and cocked her head. Her mouth opened to speak, then slowly shut.

"Yeah, it's complicated." I winced. "Crow's in town, too. Can I come in?"

She glanced over her shoulder and didn't answer.

She was alone.

Got it.

"It's all right," I said. "I don't need to come in. I'll wait outside for whoever gets here next and—"

"No, it's okay," Adele gestured me in, and I followed. She turned. "Do I get to go first?"

"Yeah."

"Why are you and Crow following us?"

"Straight to it. Good approach." I looked around the vacant house. "I'm going to tell you some things, and I'm hoping you don't hate me or Crow. Actually, you can hate me, just not Crow; well, feel free to hate Crow, but get over it quick, because—"

"Shane!"

"Right. Crow thought you might be in trouble out here on your own."

"But I'm not alone. I'm with Will."

I gazed at the floor.

"Oh, Crow." Adele exhaled hard. "All these years and she's still protecting me. Wait, how did she know we'd come here?"

I winced and raised the notebook, handed it to her.

She leafed through it. "Now I am mad at her."

I winced again. "I asked her to do it."

"Now I'm mad at you."

"You don't work with Will. You don't see the Jekyll and Hyde, how different he is when he's not around you. I guess you can take that as a compliment." I pointed at the notebook. "The Will I work with, that Crow sees, isn't a Will you'd trust with anyone."

Adele's eyes flared. "That's my decision to make!"

I backed toward the door. "I see that now. Addy, I'm leaving. I won't bother you anymore. I never meant to smother you. Not when we were young, not now."

She took a step back. "You sound like Shane, but you speak like my sister. How do you know about that? Did Crow tell you?"

I gazed at Addy and sighed. Sadie was right. Addy was fine. She made it. She didn't need me to undo her life. She only needed me to let her live it. I opened the door and stepped out. "I'll leave you be."

"If you wait . . ."

I turned and peeked at Adele. She continued, "You can apologize to Will. He ran to town to see if he could find a present for his dad, it being Christmas and all. He didn't want to go home without a present. I don't quite get it." She gestured around the place. "He said he used to live here, that the key was beneath the rock by the church. It was, but obviously the place is deserted. I'd appreciate the company."

"I don't."

The voice was deep and metered, as if each word had been weighed and measured for effect. Behind me stood a distinguished version of Will. His dad, there was no doubt.

I reached out my hand. "Shane Owen. And this is Adele Raine."

He looked at my hand but did not grasp it. "How long have you been here?"

"We just arrived." Adele stepped forward. "I was looking for you."

"Christmas service has ended. We hold that service next door. In the church." He pointed over his shoulder. "Now, if you'll kindly vacate church property, it will spare us the inconvenience of a holiday call to Officer Blake."

"We've come a long way," I said. "All four of us, including Crow and your son."

Shock hits men in a multitude of ways—rarely tears, I think, but that is exactly what happened this time. The man standing in front of us burst into tears, rocked a bit so that I grabbed his arm to steady him. He did not resist.

"Will's come home? How does he look?"

Adele smiled, "Really good. We're waiting for him now."

"Tell me where he is." The reverend grabbed my arm. "I've waited for this day long enough." He sniffed and took off his coat, then put it back on. "I will not wait another minute. Where is he?"

"I'm not exactly sure. Somewhere in town," Adele said, "He felt he needed a gift before he could come home."

This pulled another sob from the pastor.

I stared into the eyes of a father in love, a man so desperate for his son he could not think straight. Standing there fixed my own purpose. With the last whispers of my walkabout, I knew what I needed to do.

I toyed with the locket.

Please, God, just a little more time.

"Come with me." Reverend Kroft ran out the door and toward the church parking lot—I believe we left the house door wide open—and soon we were speeding, yes, speeding, toward Morneau. Ten minutes later, we arrived, and the next set of events will stay with me forever.

Picture in your mind an empty town, maybe a scene from a Western just before the outlaw gang rides in. Remove the dust and the saloon and the little kid hiding under the stagecoach and cover everything with snow and light. Morneau, decked out for Christmas. Angels blowing bugles and evergreen wreaths hung from each streetlight along the town's main street.

The road was silent. Not horror movie silent, holiday

silent. There's a difference. One says, 'Something is coming,' the other, 'Something has come.' The street was still and quiet.

In the middle of the road on the town's south side sat a young man. His back was to Morneau, and he faced out toward the miles of nothingness stretched out before him. His borrowed suit hung crumpled on his frame, and his head drooped buried in his hands. In front of him, toppled in the street, rested two jugs of orange Gatorade, green ribbons around each one.

Like a mannequin, he did not shift or flinch at the sound of our car engine; he was not in this world. He sat waiting, I think, for an imaginary bus to arrive at an imaginary bus stop and ship him south to the Twin Cities. But I wager that no such vehicle ever passed through Morneau, and certainly not on Christmas.

Leave him, if you will, and pan north on Main, past Casey's Pizza and Percy's Tire Repair. Beyond the bakery and the three-story hardware, the last business on the west side. If you stared the opposite direction down Main Street, you saw the back of a statue, a girl, carved from darkest obsidian. She, too, plunked in the middle of the road, her back to the town and to Will.

She sat cross-legged, posture erect, her backpack in front of her, waiting, I believe, to freeze, and yes, to die. Witness Crow.

The pastor slowed his car and pulled to the curb right between them.

"Who are they?" He glanced left, and then right. "Looks like they just finished a gun fight."

"That might not be far from the truth." I shared a wondering look with Adele. "Reverend Kroft, that young man slumped on the far side is yours." I puffed out air and faced Crow. "This young lady is mine to deal with."

The reverend bolted from his car and ran toward Will. Upon hearing the door slam, Will slowly rose, and I could tell he gave thought to flight. But his shoulders heaved, he reached down, and weakly lifted the Gatorades toward his approaching father, who slowed, took them, dropped them, and gave young Will a hug so real I felt its meaning from down the street. And they cried and then they laughed; then Adele joined them, and they laughed and they cried some more.

I closed my eyes at the sight of their reunion.

⌐

"What a fool you made of us." Mom didn't turn. "How many notes are there in that recital piece? Maybe twenty? How can you forget twenty notes?"

I swallowed hard. "I'm sorry."

"It is very easy to forget twenty notes," Dad interrupted. "You recovered magnificently."

"With your help." Mom hissed. "You know how Dr. Jude feels about your constantly coming to Crow's rescue."

"I know how Dr. Jude feels about too many things." Dad shot Mom a glance. "But that man will never know Coraline. My daughter analyzes every word she reads, feels every note she hears, even the missed ones."

"Save your philosophical garbage and take me home." Mom stared out the window.

Dad turned, gazed at me, and pulled the car onto the shoulder.

"What are you doing? Flat tire?" Mom asked.

"Flattened heart." Dad whispered. He removed a CD, my practice CD with a full orchestra playing "Mary Had a Little Lamb." He punched it in, turned up the volume, and stepped out of the car. He opened my car door, reached for my hand, and led me safely into the grass.

"My darling Coraline. No matter what happens in the next few days, always remember that together, we play superbly. Will you dance with me?"

He rounded my tiny waist with his hand, took hold of my other hand, and for the next forever, we danced. Cars flew by, Mom's voice rose in the distance, but nothing mattered but my gentle twirl and the gleam in Daddy's eyes. And I laughed. And he cried.

Opening my eyes to look again at Will, it struck me: there is not much difference between saying good-bye and saying hello.

~

Crow hadn't shifted. I approached her, eased down in front, and assumed her position.

"Do not say one word." Crow whispered. "I asked at the station. I know the letter is true. I know he is who he said he is. But none of that changes what he might do to her. I heard it. I heard it clearly."

I nodded. "I believe you." I reached out my hand, and she narrowed her eyes. "Yep, I'm asking you to trust me. I'm asking you to let me take you home."

Her body shook and softened. Her shoulders drooped. "If I stay, I die. If I let her go, I die. I have nothing of my own to go home to. I'm nothing."

I sat in silence before the truth. Her truth. My truth. She finally got it, and it hit me like a hammer. My walkabout hadn't given me a second chance to live. It gave me a first chance. And the moments were fleeting.

"I don't think trains run today," I said, "but we need to get you home."

Crow stared with no hardness in the eyes. They were soft and open and longing for a reason to get up off the street.

I peeked over her shoulder at the reunion still happening at the far end of town, and I glanced back at the reverend's car.

"I think I know a way back."

She took my hands, held them up to her mouth, and blew. Warmth I didn't know I had surrounded my fingers.

"I trust you."

CHAPTER 24

THE THOUGHTS OF C. RAINE

I know well what I am fleeing from
but not what I am in search of.
Michel de Montaigne

THE REVEREND DID INDEED LOAN ME HIS CAR on the promise that it would be returned sooner than later. Crow slumped into the passenger's side and shut the door, while I stood outside and shook Will's hand.

"I don't imagine I'll be seeing you again," I said.

Will glanced nervously at his dad. "Don't count on it. There are still things I need to figure out." He stepped nearer. "You'll take care of Mr. L? He's a good guy."

"Yeah, I got it." I turned and hugged Adele. "And what happens to you?"

She peeked at Will, and then gazed back at me. "I don't know. I'll call my mom and let her know I'm fine. Don't tell her I'm here. Let me go home on my own time. Maybe when you come back with the car, we can head back together." Addy bent over and knocked on the car window. Crow slid lower in the seat.

Addy straightened and grabbed my forearm. "You'll take care of her? I don't know what I'd do without her."

Honesty was all I owned, so I forced a smile and said nothing.

Soon, Crow and I sped silently south. I remembered Sadie's gag order, but here in the car I battled to contain the truth. Crow looked at peace. She was oh so close to believing, to accepting that Will might not be the monster she'd heard he was. The Crow beside me was a vast improvement over any Crow I'd been. This Crow trusted. She trusted another person . . . me. The first time around, the train struck before I ever crossed that track.

No, I wasn't here to change the future, but if I could give Crow even the slightest push, if she let Will off the hook, there wouldn't have to be a crash, there'd be no death, no red locket, no Lifeless.

"Do you think it's possible that Will might be all the way good?" I breathed deeply. "And maybe Mel is all the way bad?"

"You're talking about one of my best friends. You're saying she made up the story and spread it around just to hurt me. Why would she do that?"

We peeked at each other.

"I suppose"—my hands clutched and reclutched the wheel—"that if you both wanted the same thing."

"Yeah." She rubbed her hands back and forth across her black jeans.

A half hour of deep silence settled down between us. Crow fought through it.

"I don't want that thing, you know."

I lifted my eyebrows. "That's good." I snuck a peek at my locket, half expecting to see a bright green glow. I mean, she got it. She knew what happened. She must see through it all now.

Instead, all that remained was dull crimson, and a wave of dizziness blurred my vision.

"Crow, I don't want to take you home."

"I don't want you to." She straightened. "But I can't bear Basil's mom right now, and I'm sorry, I'm not ready for your place."

"No." I blinked hard. "I get that. But I need to show you something, and it has to be today."

I slipped out the scrap of paper Sadie gave me and looked at the address. I took a deep breath. What a fool I'd been, so focused on past events. Stop Mayday. Stop Mayday. No longer—I just wanted to reach the address in time.

—

"You think I should be locked up?"

We pulled to the curb, where Crow stared at the imposing doors of Minnesota State Hospital.

I pushed my hand through my hair. "No, there's someone I need to see, and I think he may be in here."

"You have a friend who lives here?" Crow asked.

I hope so.

I checked the address etched in granite, 576 Wabash Street, and felt nauseous. "Will you come with me?"

She didn't say a word. Crow simply pushed out into the cold, and together we climbed the steps and slipped inside.

A weighty darkness descends when you walk into a locked facility. You know the place isn't your home, but a voice deep inside says, "You're just one bad mistake from your new address, my friend."

Buzzers and buttons and the clanking of doors ushered us farther from fresh air and life. Whoever lived in here had truly left this world, and the thought of its being my father set my heart throbbing.

We reached the reception area. The sparse group of Christmas staff huddled behind a floor-to-ceiling Plexiglas wall. They were in the midst of Christmas poker. In the distance, a frightful scream, but I don't think they heard. I knocked on the glass, and the largest man looked my way and lay down his hand. The others pushed back from the table and threw their cards into a heap.

The man, Joe by his name badge, approached and reached

for the buzzer. Though bouncer huge, his voice rattled small and tinny inside my head. "May I help you?"

"Yeah, I'm looking for Cameron Raine."

This is when I was mighty glad we were in a locked facility, or I would have lost Crow. She backpedaled to the metal door and tugged.

The guy behind the glass watched her. "Your friend okay? You know, this is a state hospital, not a drop-off site. There are admission procedures."

"No, she's fine." *More or less.* "Just wants to see her dad. Is Cameron Raine here?"

"Cameron? A dad? Yeah, he's here."

Crow stopped tugging and slumped to the floor. "Dad lives here. My dad lives here?"

I shrugged and swallowed hard. I was thinking the same thing.

In one of her saner moments, Mom had told me about her wedding to Cameron Fillmore Raine.

"Marriage is a gamble, pure and simple. You think you know this man. He's been on his best behavior while you dated, and you've spent half your energy trying to figure out if it's an act or if he's for real."

"Which one was Dad?"

Mom's face turned wistful. A rare, gentle moment.

"There's nothing false in your father. He cared so much, he wilted. I watched him stop for motorists and empty pockets for every hustler on the street. If he saw a cardboard sign, there went your allowance. 'What if he's a vet? What if she hasn't eaten in days?' At some point, a man has to insulate himself, or the weight of the world crushes him. Your father could not do that. He let everyone in. Way in. I knew it before I took the walk—that he would be frail. But I thought a man frail from love was a better deal than a hard man unable to share his heart.

"Still, you walk down the aisle, face covered, wondering, Who will I see when he lifts the veil. Same guy?"

Joe whistled and twirled his keys as he walked down the hall. Doors, solid, save for a small window of reinforced glass, lined the left and the right. My father lived behind one of them.

Crow and I followed at a distance. "Shane, how did you know? I didn't know. And why?" she whispered.

Because any moment I could disappear from your life again. If you don't make a different choice, in a few months you'll disappear, too. We need to see him. Both of us.

"I'm not sure," I said. "He's alone on Christmas."

Joe stopped at a gray door on the left. "You're really family? He's never had a visitor before."

"We didn't know where he was. How long has he been here?"

"At least eight years. He was here when I came."

Crow stepped to the window. "He's been alone in a room for over eight years?"

"Cam gets out. He likes to walk the courtyard. He likes it quiet, to read or listen to music or think. Now, I'll be outside this here door, but I'll be watching. Just wanted you to know. One of you at a time."

"Crow?" I asked. "I should have told you, but I wasn't sure you'd—"

"I want in." She pressed her nose to the glass.

Joe inserted the key with a click, and the door swung open. He cleared his throat. "Cam? Look what Santa brought. A few Christmas visitors. Do you recognize this young lady? Crow. Her name's Crow. She says she's family. Do you know—" The door shut behind them, and soon Joe reappeared. I strained and listened, but could hear no sound from inside the room.

Minutes turned into an hour, and still Joe hogged the window. How I wanted to watch, but it wasn't my place.

"Well, I'll be," he whispered. "Would you look at that? She hasn't seen her dad in eight years?" Joe asked.

"Thirteen."

"It's a beautiful sight, but what kind of person lets her dad sit in here for thirteen years? Just sayin'."

Me.

Finally, Crow knocked and walked out, clutching a large book. She'd been crying, but she walked up to me and kissed my cheek. I do not know what was said in that room, but I have a feeling it bordered on the holy.

"Do I get a turn?" I grabbed Joe's forearm.

He stared at my fingers and frowned. "Cam may be worn out, but I can ask."

"Great." I slowly released him. "That's great. My name's Shane."

Joe stepped into the room again. "Cam? I have a Shane out here."

"It's Christmas. Let everyone in."

Joe popped his head out through the doorway. "I think he's getting confused. Keep it short."

I stepped into the room with thoughts of Alcatraz floating through my head. Toilet, sink, cot. That picture quickly vanished.

Books filled the room, their stacks towering to the ceiling. Kant, Kierkegaard, Plato. My eyes burned when I saw them.

Dad.

A spacious window and plenty of sun kept alive several large potted plants. An Oriental rug covered the floor. And in a rocker sat a man, hands folded, eyes filled with tears. Though crying, he did not look weak.

"You're not who I expected." He smiled. "Did you come with Coraline?"

"We're together."

He straightened and pointed to the floor. I lowered myself down at my dad's feet and let him stare. It wasn't the crazed stare I feared, but a controlled stare, a settled stare, which, oddly enough, causes fear as well.

"Shane." Dad looked off. "I need to know. Is Coraline well?"

"I think she's coming around, but life's been hard on her."

Dad stopped rocking. "For how long?"

"Thirteen years."

He nodded. "I sensed that. She wouldn't answer all my questions."

My locket. I could feel its weight, its change. "Da— Mr. Raine. Do you believe in second chances?"

"In some cases. I just got one with Coraline. She promised to bring Addy." He slapped the armrests of his rocker. "For years a man sits in a chair, or walks through a courtyard, wishing he was something different, something more, something other than an agent of pain, and then what he most fears and most desires walks in the door."

I rose to my knees in front of him. "I'm not sure I have

much time. But I need to hear this: Why did you leave Crow?"

"She wanted to ask me that. She couldn't." He looked down. "This place robs one of all pride. I have no problem telling you." He breathed deep. "I was a weak man, Shane. I loved Coraline and Addy and their mother so much. I didn't want any of them growing old nursing a troubled father. I know that makes no sense, and I know now that they needed me. I was selfish." He glanced around. "But I've paid. I fear everyone has paid."

"You didn't leave *because* of Crow?"

He shook his head. "She's the reason I stayed as long as I did."

Oh, Dad, tell Crow. Tell her that straight.

I grabbed his arm. "Then go back. Leave this place and go back. Hug Addy and walk with Crow and talk sense when they're all turned around."

His jaw tightened. "Who are you to say?"

I dug in my pocket and pulled out the locket. Crimson faintly flickered, and I held it up.

"Crow wants you back, very much. She's about to make some choices you can't affect from in here. I need you where she is. She needs you where she is. I don't know what to do about Jude, but I need you out of this room and into her life and—"

Black. The locket went black, and my vision blurred.

I tried to stand, but my knees buckled. I fell forward into Dad's lap, and he stroked my hair.

"Addy loves you. I still love you, Dad. I'm so sorry I screamed so loudly."

My voice changed. It became younger, higher, and through double vision I saw his strong arms wrap around my five-year-old ones. "I'll play my song better next time. Don't leave, Daddy."

"Coraline?" He leaned forward and rocked and rocked. I felt his embrace, gentle and warm. And then I didn't. I passed through Dad, frantic and standing. "Where are you, Coraline?"

Lying on the floor, Daddy.

In the distance, the door opened. "Are you all right, Cam?"

"I want my girl back!" Dad sobbed. "She was right here. Two seconds ago, my girl was right here!"

"I'm here." Crow ran in and threw herself into his arms. He blinked his eyes, stared around the room, and embraced her.

"I'm right here, Dad. I've missed you. Oh, God, I've missed you and failed you, but I'm not leaving, you got that? I'm not leaving you, and you're not staying here."

"You never failed me," Dad said, his voice cracking. "I failed you."

And I felt it, a tug across the middle, pulling, pulling. I didn't fight it.

I'd done what I could.

My walkabout was over.

I emerged from the dream, the scene slipping away from me. My dad's broken voice—"I love you, Coraline"—the last words I heard.

CHAPTER 25

THE THOUGHTS OF C. RAINE

*Death is not extinguishing the light; it is only
putting out the lamp because the dawn has come.*
Rabindranath Tagore

I OPENED MY EYES IN THE CORNER OF LIFELESS'S ROOM. I wasn't
alone. The room was filled with people standing around
the bed. This included the regulars—Dr. Ambrose,
Nurse Latte, and Adele—but also a host of faces new to
the setting: Mom and Jude, Mr. Loumans and a tearful
Thomas, and Mr. Kroft and Will, who was sitting up in a
wheelchair.

And my dad.

I pushed my way to the bedside. My body looked the
same.

"No. No." I stroked her head with an unfeeling hand.
"You can't be here. You can't still be here. What did you do
to Will?" My voice lowered. "He's a good kid. I know you
believed me. Why couldn't you let it go?"

Will's dad cleared his throat. "I confess to you all that I've never done anything quite like this before, and it breaks my heart."

I glanced around at the faces. At the sniffles and tears and the machine, which had been moved out from the wall. I knew what this was.

"You can't do this to her! She dreams! Of green fields and the yellow sun." I broke down and crumpled beside the bed. "I have dreams."

"Her life touched each of ours. Without her, we will not be the same, but because of her, we've all been changed."

But nothing's changed.

"Oh, I wouldn't be so sure." Sadie stood next to me, knitting needles at her side.

"But the car." I rose. "It still hit the train."

"Yes, it did. One horrible moment in time." She eased close to my ear. "But a different moment. One you couldn't control.

"Crow . . . you wasn't driving."

I frowned, opened my mouth to speak, and frowned again.

"Don't look so surprised. You and Thomas, Will and Addy couldn't all fit up front." Sadie raised her eyebrows. "You, my dear Coraline, was in the backseat."

"No, that's not true. I remember."

"You remember the first time around." Sadie hesitated. "Mayday came, done its dirty work. Nothing you done on your walkabout could change that. But you sure 'nuff changed *you*. I wish you could've seen yourself that last night. Prettiest yellow dress I ever laid eyes on."

"Yellow? I don't understand."

Sadie grinned. "You and Addy decided you should step out in the same dress. Truth be your dad thought it a fine idea, and since he was payin'. And your dates, Thomas and Will, did they not look handsome in them black suits? Um, hmm."

"Wait. Thomas? *I* went to prom. In a yellow dress. With Thomas Loumans?"

"And a fine time the four of you had right until the end, until that big old nasty train clipped the driver's-side rear. You got the worst of it. Thomas and Addy, barely a scratch."

Deep inside it started. A chuckle that gained strength and volume and turned into a laugh, clear and free. Thomas. I had dated Thomas. My spirit bore witness it was true. I walked over to him, felt that strange blending of joy and pain, and kissed his cheek. Did he feel it? Did I feel it? No. But it was real just the same.

"You don't need to see this, Coraline." Sadie gestured me back.

"Is this really—"

"It's an end, so it has been decided by those legally involved. But I reckon, for you, bound now by a different law, this may also be a beginning."

I ran through Jude and stroked Addy's hair. "Can't I touch them?" I dashed to Dad. "One more time. Let them know I'm here."

"No, child." Sadie pointed out the door. "But you can now leave."

I breathed deeply. "I won't get pulled back?"

Sadie smiled.

"Where will I go?"

"Some things aren't for me to know. Some of us only work this side. But now that the walkabout be done, you are tied to nothing that was. Not even bad decisions."

I followed her around the bed, my hand outstretched to each one I passed. I reached Jude and paused.

"Leave him go, Coraline. Leave him go. For your own sake. Bitterness be a poor partner wherever you're heading."

My breathing quickened, and my hands shook. "How do I get free of him?"

"Choose it. Give him over." Sadie stepped toward Jude, her eyes blazing. "Justice will be served on the man. Just not by you." Sadie faced me square. "Do you believe me?"

I closed my eyes and pictured my knife in hand.

"He deserves to die," I whispered.

"Yes, child, he does."

I squeezed tight my fists then opened them, and in my mind the knife clattered to the floor. "You promise justice will be served?"

Sadie's face softened.

"Then, I'm ready," I said.

Sadie bowed, and together we reached the door. Behind me, the steady beep changed to a solid tone. I glanced over my shoulder as both Adele and Dad wrapped me in their embrace.

"Tell me, Sadie. Did Crow ever, did I ever, did Dad ever find out how much I loved him? You were there my last months. I don't know what happened. Did I do any better?"

Sadie sighed, and a tear fell. "You done took plenty of courtyard walks with your father, and let him know all he needed to hear. Shoot, you saw him most every day. Long after visiting hours ended, you two night owls stayed up, talking that strange philosophical language only you shared." She wiped her nose with a mitten. "Yeah, I'd say you told him everything. You done good."

I breathed deep and nodded. "So that's it? I just leave and . . . wait." I pulled out the locket and walked over to my body. Amid the tears and hugs, I bent down and clasped the necklace around my neck. "It looks good on you." I whispered, "Thank you."

I rejoined Sadie at the door and took one last look. Dad's voice rose over the din. "I didn't notice it on her before."

The halls of the hospital vanished, and once again

Sadie and I stood where we'd met, next to the last of three ambulances. Only this time, there was no flashing red, no yellow tape, no police blue. There was no grisly crash. Just three ambulances, parked like limousines in the middle of a field.

"My dear Crow. This is our good-bye." She tapped the side-view mirror. "Need proof you done good?" I leaned and stared and touched and then stroked my face.

I was beautiful.

She continued, "I could tell you much more about the weeks before Mayday. But it don't matter now." She hugged me hard. "Oh, child. That twisted soul that was you is gone. Look at you!" She swatted my backside. "Now go on. Your ride be waitin'."

Sadie gazed at the first ambulance, no longer filled with fog but with light.

I walked quickly toward it. Thinking back, I should have thanked Sadie, but if you've ever felt the excitement of the future, if you've ever collided with hope, you understand you don't retrace your steps. I hopped inside the cab and soaked in the warmth. It didn't take long to locate a pen and my notebook.

Which brings me back to now, whenever that is.

⌣

It's been done. I've finished the course and set the record straight. Will this be read? Will the story of any of our lives be read or remembered? That's a good question, one that never came up in philosophy class, too busy were we discussing global warming. I have no definitive answer. All I know is that someday every page gets written, and until someday comes, the ending can be changed, and even the craziest dreams have a chance.

I mean, look at me; I'm writing after all.

Wait. Hold on. The ambulance is moving. The windows are down, and the wind blows gently across my face.

The fields are green and alive. Alive with laughter.

Oh, it's good. . . .

READ THE AWARD-WINNING NOVEL
FROM JONATHAN FRIESEN—
JERK, CALIFORNIA

"EMOTIONALLY REWARDING AND EFFECTIVE."
—*VOYA*

TEXT © JONATHAN FRIESEN

chapter one

"SAM HAS IT. QUESTION IS, HOW BAD?"

The pediatrician smiled. Like he got off on destroying a kid's life. Like children frequently went to sleep normal and woke up monsters who couldn't keep their damn bodies still.

He stared at me, waiting. My right hand twitched. He pointed and continued. "The disease has seasons. One day he'll flail like a windmill in spring. Then the wind'll die and you won't see anything for months." He turned to my mom. "There are some experimental drugs—"

"Who the hell is supposed to pay for those?" my stepdad said.

The doctor rose. "I can see you need some time, Bill." He shook my six-year-old hand, gave my stepdad a pat on the back, and slipped out of the examining room, leaving the three of us to stare at my jerking hands and shoulders.

"What'd he say, Mom? Bill? When's it gonna go away?"

Bill stood and paced the room. "Go away? Your twitches won't ever stop." He cursed and kicked the doctor's swivel chair.

I stared at Mom. "Never? Not even when I'm older?"

Mom scooted her chair in front of mine. "He says you have Tourette's."

I mouthed the word, and she leaned forward and stroked my arms. Gentle at first, then harder and harder and mixed with tears. I knew she was trying to rub that bad word out of me.

"What does that mean?" I asked.

"It means," Bill said, "you can forget about ever running my machines."

My hands squeezed the jacket Bill gave me, the green one with Tar-Boy on the front and a cement mixer on the back. I pulled free of Mom and grabbed Bill's pant leg.

"I can stop it. Please, Bill." I started to cry. "I'll be still. Promise!"

Old Bill turned his back, Mom closed her eyes, and even at six years old I knew I was alone.

chapter two

"YOU'RE QUIET IN GROUP TODAY."

Leslie, the social worker, stares at me. I look around at the others. Eight guys rest their heads on the table.

"Everyone's quiet," I say.

She places her young elbows on the table and rests her young head in her young hands. "But you're somewhere else, aren't you, Sam?"

Bryan snores from across the circle, and I point at him, but this woman's eyes won't go away. I glance at the clock—ten more minutes.

"I *wish* I were somewhere else. How many more weeks do I have to come?"

Dumb question. I know exactly. Ten. In Old Bill's barn hang fourteen sheets of paper covered with smiley-face suns. Ten of those sheets aren't yet blasted through with BB-gun pellets.

Leslie smiles the smile people use at funerals. "One of the

ways we build friendships is by answering questions. A good way to do this is through small talk. You respond with something cheery about your day or your family."

Room 14 is a morgue. Powder-blue walls and no window. Only the tick of the clock and the buzz and flicker of the fluorescent light remind me I'm still alive.

I slump down in my seat and cross my arms.

Socially maladaptive. According to the special-ed teacher, that's what I am. Sentenced to a semester in Leslie's "Sunshine Club," I'm one of the lucky ones up for parole at Christmas break.

I glance at the lifers. Ken and Kerry, autistic twins; Larry, who slugged a cook. Not sure how cramming in a tiny room for an hour after school will turn any of us into charmers.

The word *maladaptive* scrawled in invisible ink across my forehead just stole another hour of my life. Today, I don't have the time.

"I can see you're defensive, but look around you, Sam." Leslie's eyes plead. "These boys are here to be your friends."

Another snore from Bryan.

"Let's try a role-play. I'll pretend I like you." She perks up and clears her throat. "Remember, small talk. Answer with something general and light." Her smile widens, so do her eyes. "I'd love to hear something about your family."

I check the clock, look back at her, and nod. "My dad is dead. Don't worry about it, because he was a loser drunk who dug holes for a living. But he was generous. Kind enough to leave me this damn disease as my inheritance."

Leslie's smile is gone, her face frozen.

I push back from the table. "He left my mom for some other gal and then got himself killed." I stand. "And his replacement, Old Bill, is almost as bad. Any other questions?" I pick up my backpack and walk to the door. "Do appreciate the small-talk lesson."

Bryan's snore catches on something ugly, and he wakes with a "Huh!"

Before the door closes, a quieter Leslie goes to work on another victim. "You're quiet in group today, Bryan."

I jog to my locker, drop to the ground, and change into running shoes. I push through the front doors of Mitrista High. Outside, air hangs heavy, full of October mist. My lungs suck in the soup.

I stand and stretch and jog out of town. It's quiet. Birds, frogs, crickets—thick air smothers them all. The paved road ends and shoes hit gravel. My pace evens. My brain clears.

Shouldn't have come down on Leslie. Ain't her fault.

I jog through Bland—population sixteen—past three houses and Crusty's Coop, and reach tiny Pierce. It's only a minute's run from our farm on the near side of town to the Shell station here.

Two cars filling up? Today's 10K must be a bigger race than I thought.

Behind me, gravel pops and crackles, and I glance over my shoulder. Three school buses approach. I drift to the road's edge as they rumble by. A minute later, a string of twenty more overtakes me. I reluctantly fall in line behind them, and we all turn left into the Northwoods Wildlife Refuge.

The race won't start for an hour, but already a crowd gathers. I dash through the parking lot and join the onlookers beneath a string of colored pennants. I weave through the people until I reach the rope cordoning off the runners' starting area. The grassy field is littered with athletes from all over Minnesota, and above them stretches a large banner.

Northwoods 10k Off-road Classic

Kids wearing numbers small-talk easily. They laugh and stretch and check the sky.

I lean against the rope that separates me from them. I glance up, too. It will rain. It will rain hard and fast and their running shoes will stick in the mud. The sloppy path through the woods will make for a slow race. But it will be a race, and I don't have a number, and I'm on the wrong side of the rope.

A woman hands me a program with the list of runners. I scan the schools, the names. Over two hundred numbers today. I trace the list with my finger and locate the Cs. Sam Carrier would have been number thirty.

"Carrier?"

I look up. Coach Lovett approaches. Mitrista's new running coach weighs in at over three hundred pounds. But for an extra thousand a year, I guess a shop teacher will do most anything.

"From what I hear, you'd win this race. What's holdin' you

back, son?" I look over his shoulder at Mitrista's four entrants. Two shove each other; darn near a fistfight. Coach follows my gaze. "Lord knows we need ya." He turns back toward me. "Mailed you off a sports waiver. You get that signed?"

I exhale slow and kick at the dirt.

"Just need *one* of your folks' signatures," he says, and taps my shin with his shoe. Coach steps nearer and whispers. "Your stepdad never has to see it."

I blink hard, and my mouth gapes. Coach smiles.

"When I took this job from Coach Johnson, I asked him for the name of Mitrista's best runner. Don't you think that runner should be on the running team?"

"He told you about Old Bill?" I ask.

"Told me a lot of things about you. Didn't understand the half of them."

I stare down at the rope, feel the first drops of rain on the back of my neck, and nod. "Farm needs work, and he don't want me doin' extras. Besides, keepin' a secret from him ain't that easy."

Coach steps back. "Reckon not. But it's a shame to see all that speed go to waste. Think on it." He turns, takes one step back toward the team, and stops. "When it rains, that trail will be either grease or quicksand. Bad footing takes a runner down. Sure'd like to know where the slick spots are." He faces me, smiles, and leans forward. I lean in, too.

"How'd you like to give the trail a quick run? We could use a scouting report." He pats my back. "Don't need a waiver signed for that."

I straighten.

I'd be running for the team.

My hand clenches, crushes the program, and my shoulder leaps three times.

Coach takes off his cap, runs his hand through thinning hair. "What in the world is that?"

He saw. He asked. Coach Johnson must not have told him. Probably seconds until he takes back his offer. I lift the rope, duck under, and dart past him toward the trailhead.

The sky dims. Moments later, rain falls straight and hard. It lands with giant, soaking glops.

Runners dash for cover beneath the race tent. Spectators race to their cars. I stand and let water bounce off my jerking shoulder, stream off my sniffing nose. I'm in nearly constant motion. Today, like every day, seven seconds of still is all I get.

A megaphoned voice fights through the storm. "Due to weather conditions, the Northwoods 10K Classic is postponed! Race postponed!"

Whoops and groans go up from beneath the tent, and numbered kids streak back into the rain, hurdle the rope, and thunder toward waiting buses. I give my head a violent shake. I'm left alone.

Minutes pass, maybe more. Soaked cotton suctions onto my skin, but I don't want shelter. I want to feel the chill. I want to feel *something*. I spin around, watch raindrops dance in the puddles, and think how close I was to running a race.

I slosh into the starting area. The clearing is a small lake, and water licks my shoelaces. A number floats by. I scoop it up and put it on—stretch and smile like a numbered kid should. The downpour eases for a few seconds, and I can faintly make out where the course bottlenecks and disappears into the woods. With the tree cover from there on, it'd be a drier run.

In the first grouping, Sam Carrier. He holds the fastest time of any senior this year—

A splotch of red shifts against the trees. A figure stands near the entrance to the course.

I look around. Shadows mill about the tent, but that's all.

"Hey," I holler. "You probably didn't hear. They called it!"

The kid doesn't move.

I walk nearer. "You can't run this course in this rain. It washes out. Ten more minutes and they'll cancel it for today!" I squint toward the road. "Your team's probably waiting for you in the bus!"

I turn back. The guy in red is gone.

I blink hard and splash through the clearing.

Late afternoon with skies this dark? Kid'll get lost for sure.

"Hold up!" I dart in after him.

Can't be more than a few steps ahead.

I run my hard, angry run, but fifteen minutes pass and I haven't caught anyone. No way he's still in front of me. He probably never started in—

A flash of red rounds the next bend.

I push harder but don't gain.

Use your head, Carrier!

I duck onto a footpath that snakes through dense tree cover. Sticks and brambles crunch beneath my feet, and tree limbs gouge and scratch my arms. I pop out of the woods and rejoin the trail as the kid passes. He screams, startled, and races by me. It's not a boy scream.

Can't be.

I grit my teeth and pull alongside her on a straightaway through a field.

"What are you doin'?" I huff.

"I'm running a race." She speaks easily, her breath barely audible.

I'm quiet except for the squeak of my waterlogged shoes. I pick up my pace, glance to my left. Our arms bump and we reenter the woods.

"You know nobody else is?" I say.

"What?" she asks.

"Running a race."

She pulls up. I try to stop and turn, but my feet slide on a tree root. Both feet flip up, and I land on my gut in a puddle of mud. I groan, push up to my knees, and look up at her.

I watch raindrops trickle down her cheek; see them kiss her lips before continuing their path down her neck. The drops disappear behind the red shirt and shorts that cling tight against her, before they emerge and trail down her legs, drip off her body. *Lucky raindrops.*

Her body is beautiful and she runs fast and I can't remember who spoke last.

"Weren't you racing, too?" She looks at me, all of me. I wish I were covered with more mud. My opponent cocks her head, gently bites her lip.

I look down. "The sky is dark. I thought you might get lost."

She moves close. I glance up, but I'm still on my knees and I can't find an appropriate spot to put my gaze. I drop my eyes to her ankles.

Even her ankles are pretty.

"So you ran through the woods to make sure I'd stay on the trail?"

I nod.

She laughs. It's cute. "Where do you go to school?"

"Mitrista."

"Well, Mr. Mitrista, I run for Minnetonka, and I don't need your help. But I am training, and I do need these miles." She whispers, "Thanks for the push."

She reaches out her hand, but when I don't shake it, she brushes soaked hair off my forehead. My eyes close, and when I open them she's looking at her smeary brown fingers. She smiles and leans forward. Her breath is warm against my ear.

"You're muddy."

She straightens and takes off running.

I turn to watch. She stops and looks back over her shoulder. "Are you going to make it home?"

I nod my mud-caked head and point toward the ground. "I live here."

Again, she smiles.

I look down where my finger points at the mud puddle. *I live here? What kind of stupid line is that? And get up off your knees, Carrier!*

I grab a nearby limb and haul myself to my feet. "I meant that I live near here."

She's gone.

I glance around. My muscles don't jerk, and I close my eyes. I breathe deep, and like the third runner who finally catches up, the disease overtakes me. Slowly at first—a hard eyeblink. But that's not enough; there's more that has to work its way out, and my teeth grind. Movement spreads to my shoulder, and soon my whole body springs to twitchy life.

Good thing she ran off when she did.

I run through our imagined conversation start to finish.

"Hi, my name's Sam. What school do you run for? What's your name? Do you like muddy guys who talk to you from their knees?" I exhale long and hard. *Shouldn't have bolted out of that small-talk lesson.*

I stare one last time down the path where the most beautiful girl in the world had run. Then I take off my number, turn, and trudge back the way I came.

AND LOOK FOR
RUSH!

HE COULD BURN.
SHE COULD DIE.
ANYTHING FOR THE...

R U S H

JONATHAN FRIESEN
AWARD-WINNING AUTHOR OF JERK, CALIFORNIA

"FRIESEN'S THRILL RIDE BENEFITS FROM ITS UNUSUAL SETTING AND ITS PULSE-POUNDING ACTION (AND ROMANCE!), MAKING IT GO DOWN LIKE A SIX-PACK OF RED BULL." —*BOOKLIST*